Evil on the High Seas

Mrs. Lillywhite Investigates
BOOK NINE

Emily Queen

Evil on the High Seas

ISBN- 978-1-953044-75-4

First Edition

Printed in the U.S.A.

Contents

CHAPTER ONE

From across the room, Rosemary Lillywhite appeared to be having the time of her life: cheeks flushed pink, cornflower eyes bright with excitement, a smile painted scarlet across her face. Lovely, in a word, thought her admirer—lovely, indeed.

He snaked his way through the densely packed throng of partygoers to hover near his quarry and wait, patiently, in hopes her attention might turn in his direction.

It didn't take long before her gaze caught his, and the look in her eye at once both dropped his stomach to the floor and sent his heart soaring.

"Max!" the vision in silk slipped her arm through his own and reached up—not far, given the height of her heels—and kissed him on the cheek. "I thought perhaps you'd been kidnapped by one of Vera's actress friends. You all but disappeared into a cloud of taffeta!"

Rosemary's mouth turned down into a pout she knew

to be induced by heightened emotions and an excess of gin, but which she was, however, powerless to suppress. Moreover, she couldn't presume to impose any sort of limitation on Max, considering she planned to leave him in two days' time. If he wanted taffeta, she'd no right to object.

Of course, deep down, Rosemary knew Chief Inspector Maximilian Whittington had eyes only for her—a feeling that was, despite her impending departure, entirely reciprocated.

"None of those ladies hold a candle to you," Max replied smoothly, though Rosemary noticed a flicker of emotion cross his face. She turned a blind eye, determined not to let it interfere with the gallant mood, but allowed herself the pleasure of his reassurance for a few moments until they were pounced on by two more of her traveling companions.

"Rosie, darling," Vera Woolridge, Rosemary's best friend and newly named sister-in-law, drawled, "would you please inform your peasant of a brother that under no circumstances will either you or I deign to participate in simulated horse riding! I've seen photographs, and it looks positively lewd!"

Once upon a time, Rosemary might have refrained from tossing back a tart remark, but she'd discovered that becoming embroiled in murder investigation after murder investigation significantly lowered one's inhibitions. Furthermore, it gave her no end of pleasure to speak the words she knew would light Vera up hotter than a gas lamp.

"That sounds exactly like something my mother would say," Rosemary replied, sending her brother, Frederick, into near-hysterical laughter that launched a fine spray of gin into the air. To compare one's wife to one's mother was a gaffe he had unwisely made on more than one occasion.

Below a raven-sweep of hair cut sharply across her forehead, her eyes narrowed, but Vera maintained her composure. "You're quite lucky you missed me, husband dear," she retorted as Frederick sputtered, "or you would have been forced to buy me a replacement dress—and shoes, as well!"

Frederick stopped laughing quite so hard and grimaced, "I'm certain I'll have bought you half the dresses in America before we return from this holiday. In fact, we may need to travel home on a much larger ship!"

"Oh, Freddie, you foolish man," Vera purred. "Today's ocean liners have been fitted with the most spacious cargo holds; I could bring a Rolls Royce back from the States and still have room for at least fifteen trunks! That ought to be enough to lift the doldrums, don't you think?"

It was true, Vera could use a pick-me-up. Once touted

as the next big hit, her latest play had run for two nights before being shut down over a copyright dispute between the two cowriters. She'd been intent on stardom, and the whole incident had come as quite a blow. With her hopes dashed, Vera had set her sights on convincing Rosemary to come along to the States. Besides considering Rosemary's relationship with Max, it hadn't been a hard sell.

Taking pity on Vera, Rosemary weighed in against her brother and added, "I'm positive the onboard shops sell a variety of luggage, just in case one happens to arrive at the port with more to carry than when one departed."

The comment earned her a glare that didn't hold much ire given its accompanying smirk. "If the advert posters are correct, I'm certain this trip will cost nearly as much as Father hoped to spend on the American expansion project," Frederick said jovially and downed the rest of his G&T in one swallow. He had ingeniously managed to turn a leisure trip into a fact-finding mission backed by their father in hopes of taking Woolridge & Sons across the pond. The way his life and luck had been going lately, he'd succeed with flying colors. "It's all glitz and glamour—at least for the ladies. Us gents only need one trunk apiece, isn't that right, Des?"

"Speak for yourself," the fifth member of the traveling party replied, mock-seriously. "I'm simply dying over the summer lines, you know." Desmond Cooper's joke elicited the desired titter of laughter, which in turn lit his own handsome face with a smile.

The man had an easy way that drew women to him like a flower drew bees. In fact, Rosemary had fancied Desmond since before she'd begun to understand the concept of romance. It had started with the innocence of children; as a girl, she'd been attracted to his good looks, sense of humor, and charisma.

But he'd been Frederick's chum, old enough to leave her feeling immature and insignificant. When the boys went off to university, she had laid the idea of Desmond to rest. Then, she'd fallen so head-over-heels for Andrew Lillywhite that all other men ceased to exist. Every other one had paled in comparison.

He'd shined so brightly in her eyes that when, after a few short years of marriage, Andrew died, Rosemary had thought she'd never, ever love again. For over a year, she'd wallowed and, when she'd finally emerged, found herself fielding more suitors than expected. During their last—and somewhat ill-fated—holiday, Desmond had made the move she had been waiting most of her life for him to make, and she had discovered, quite unexpectedly, that it wasn't his lips she craved after all!

It seemed a cruel twist of fate for Maximilian Whittington to have been the next to capture her heart;

after all, he had been Andrew's closest friend. The rumor mill, if given half a chance, would chew them up and spit them out. Throw in Rosemary's penchant for involving herself in Max's murder investigations, and well, it was a miracle they hadn't yet been publicly roasted. While Rosemary couldn't give a fig about the opinions of strangers, her family's—and Max's—reputations were another story.

"Tell us more about your travel plans," one of Frederick's workmates urged, bringing Rosemary out of her reverie with a snap. "Which ship did you choose?"

As her brother puffed up his chest and prepared to answer, Desmond interrupted.

"That's what they call a loaded question," he replied, sending an elbow jab towards Frederick's chest that distracted his friend long enough to allow Desmond center stage. "We've spent more time deciding on a vessel than we'll spend on board! Old Freddie wanted to cruise with the Americans until he realized it's not just the last three miles you can't drink—it's the whole way across! Dry ships, indeed. What fun would that be?"

Frederick elbowed Desmond back for real, harder than he might have under normal circumstances but certainly not as hard as he ever had during their lifelong friendship, and made a correction. "In point of fact, I ultimately came down on the side of the French. Their newest liners are touted as the most luxurious: fit for a queen such as my gorgeous wife!"

The comment softened Vera's face into the indulgent smile she wore whenever Frederick's eyes were on her, the subtle shift surprising Rosemary even though she ought to have been used to it. Her brother and dear friend had fought their attraction to one another for so long that sometimes she was still shocked they'd finally admitted it, much less taken marriage vows!

"However, I was outvoted," Frederick complained. "The ladies are, evidently, highly patriotic and insisted upon the Cunard Line. To merry old England!" He lifted his glass and toasted the room, the joviality falling flat for one man—a man whose hopes and plans were being dashed like waves against a rocky shore: a fitting, if clichéd metaphor for one who couldn't bear the thought of his beloved sailing away without the promise she'd return feeling the same way about him as she seemed to do now.

"If the *Ile de France* were finished," Vera retorted, "we might have agreed with you, darling. *She* might have been worth the trouble."

Max's brow furrowed, so Rosemary stepped in to explain. "The French liners are beautifully decorated, and they have the best dining, but we've been warned the staff is let's simply say less accommodating than that of the British ships."

"Which, of course, precludes the American option,"

Frederick joked. "They've already proved they don't take kindly to taking orders from us Brits!"

While Desmond laughed heartily, Vera raised an eyebrow and said dryly, "They're sure to adore you in the States, darling, with that attitude."

"I predict he'll be banished back to London within a fortnight." Desmond got in one last jab.

Frederick merely smiled and replied, "Not so, old boy. I predict a rousing success; in fact, this holiday could, theoretically, extend for quite some time."

The man in waiting—the one who couldn't stop thinking about what he had to lose, started. He'd been under the impression this holiday would last a fortnight or a month at most—the phrase "extend for quite some time" sent an icy shiver up his spine. How long might it take for his love to find herself fancying another?

"So, the day after tomorrow, we—myself, Vera, Rosemary, and Desmond," Frederick continued, "will set sail from Southampton, en route to New York City aboard the RMS—"

Having finally summoned his nerves, the nervous man made a snap decision, his voice rising above the din and surprising himself along with the rest of the room. "Excuse me," Constable Morris Clayton interrupted, tapping his cuff link against his glass until someone lowered the music's volume. He ignored his inspector's curiously cocked eyebrow (Max had no idea what

Clayton was up to; one could never tell with that lad!) and forged on, "I don't mean to be rude, but I've something of an announcement to make—or, rather, a question to ask."

The constable was a young chap whose eagerness to please grated on Max's nerves daily, yet who had earned himself top marks for his ability to stay calm under pressure. Rosemary adored him for recently having helped her out of a painful jam during a murder investigation and also for his gentle treatment of Anna, her sweet young lady's maid, and the object of his affections.

The object of his attention, now, as well, for his eyes found hers in the crowd and did not waver.

"Anna, I'm well and truly convinced you're the one for me," Clayton professed to the stunned young woman. "Before you sail off and are stolen away by some attractive American—will you marry me?" The constable pulled a small box from his coat pocket, proving his question was more than a mere whim, and dropped to one knee.

Anna let out a squeal that made Rosemary's eyes water and rushed forward into his arms. "Yes! Of course!"

He swept her towards him, but before he had a chance to plant a kiss on her lips, the room went up in a chorus of hurrahs, and he seemed to lose his nerve. Anna's lips met the distance between them enthusiastically; young Clayton's cheeks burned ruddy, and with that, they hurried off towards the entrance hall and some much-needed privacy.

"Who would have thought he'd have the nerve?" Frederick commented with admiration.

"He would have been daft to let Anna slip away," Rosemary replied, receiving a murmur of agreement from Vera and a grunt from Max, who muttered something about consequences if his constable were to ever bring any harm to his new bride.

It was a sentiment echoed by all.

Chapter Two

Much later, after the last of the guests had been tucked into cabs or wandered on home, Rosemary yawned and lowered herself onto the settee next to Max. "Are you sure you're all right with this?" Rosemary asked for at least the dozenth time since the subject of America had been broached.

Max sighed and shifted until his deep brown eyes met hers. "Couples do it all the time, spend time apart. It doesn't have to signify the end of anything. Not unless you want it to."

He fished a pack of matches out of his pocket and lit a cigarette. The smoke curled languidly, obscuring his face for a long moment before he blew out a forceful exhale and reappeared from the cloud with a pensive expression. "But if you want me to say I'm thrilled you'll be gone for the next several weeks or months— off again to spend your time with a man who is entirely enamored of you—it would be a blatant lie."

The conviction in his voice made Rosemary's heart skip a beat. Her choice to travel had nothing to do with a lingering fixation on Desmond, nor was she purposely running from Max. At least, she didn't think she was.

If she were being honest, Rosemary would have to admit there had been an underlying tension between the two of them lately—mostly regarding her inability to keep out of his murder investigations or, more specifically, her lack of remorse for doing so.

Recently, she had begun to wonder if they were right for one another yet couldn't bear the thought of saying the words aloud. It wasn't her feelings she doubted, but their compatibility, and it felt like the twist of a knife to her heart.

"Why don't you come along?" She ignored his comment about Desmond and offered, even though she knew what the answer would be. Max had only briefly contemplated the idea the first time she'd asked and had ultimately decided a summer abroad wasn't enough to tear him away from his work, no matter how enticing.

He had not wavered from his choice, even though accepting the invitation would foil what he considered an underhanded attempt on Desmond's part to weasel his way even further into Rosemary's life.

Anything but naive, Rosemary had considered the possibility but simply decided that since Desmond's feelings, if they still existed, were unrequited, they were also irrelevant. Complicated, yes, given their history and connections; even though she didn't want to be with him in a romantic way, Rosemary still adored Desmond as a friend and trusted him like family.

She'd been just as surprised as Frederick and Vera at his unexpected return, intrigued by his tales of a merry band of friends he'd met in New York City and impressed by his success in solving a murder investigation with their help.

Max still had his doubts, truth be told, especially given that Desmond had bragged and also simultaneously failed to tell the thrilling tale in its entirety. Rosemary suspected he was waiting for his chance to do so in dramatic fashion, perhaps not until their arrival in the States, but Max wasn't so charitable.

Regardless, the group—sans Max—had enthusiastically agreed to make the transatlantic journey, something Rosemary and Frederick had often wondered if they'd ever have a chance to do. In fact, how her brother had managed to get it past their mother, Rosemary couldn't imagine. Evelyn Woolridge was so convinced they would all perish at sea that she'd carefully checked the family burial vault and, Rosemary suspected, lit a candle to ward off the Kraken.

"You know I can't go with you, Rosemary," Max said and stubbed the cigarette out, hard. "I have a job, a responsibility. I can't flit off at the drop of a hat."

He waved a hand dismissively, and Rosemary felt her hackles rise as they always did when the conversation reached this point. "I'm not flitting off, Max." Perhaps she was, but it was her prerogative to flit, wasn't it? To live life while she was still young enough to enjoy it?

"You know that's not what I meant," he said, his voice softening. "You're a woman of means, Rosemary. Of leisure, and you should enjoy all that entails, including seeing the world. I would never tell you not to follow your heart—wherever it may take you."

That his finances might play a role in Max's decline had occurred to Rosemary, but the offer to cover his portion of the trip had died on her lips. He might not be a man of significant means, but he was one who knew the value of hard work and, of course, a prideful man.

"I do know that," she replied sincerely. "And I understand your choice to decline."

Max tipped a finger under her chin and looked deep into her eyes. "I'm not sure you do, but what will be, will be. And what I'll be is sorely disappointed if you don't come back feeling the same way about me as I do about you."

It was impossible to stay angry with the man, which was fine with her. Rosemary leaned in, thinking she couldn't imagine feeling any differently than she did at that moment. It was easy to ignore the niggling worry in her head that told her the toll of time and space was only measurable upon one's return from the journey.

CHAPTER THREE

When Anna arrived the following morning to assist with the final round of packing and preparation for the journey, Rosemary had already been up for hours. Even sated with gin, she'd hardly slept, her thoughts swinging back and forth like a pendulum, each oscillation a question.

Would Max wait for her, and was it fair to ask him to? *Swish.* Would time apart serve to cement their love, or would the separation ultimately destroy it? *Swoosh.* Would the journey be smooth and the seas calm, or was she destined to, as her mother predicted, meet her end in the middle of the Atlantic Ocean? *Swish.* Did the tensions between herself and Max qualify as insurmountable, or was she merely afraid of loving someone enough to potentially find herself devastated by another loss? *SWOOSH.*

So focused was she that Rosemary hardly noticed Anna's red-rimmed eyes and downturned lips, at least not for a few more moments than would have been considered polite. When she finally noted the girl's appearance, her brow furrowed, and she immediately forgot her own worries.

"Oh no, dear, what's the trouble?" Rosemary asked, moving a pile of dresses to make room on the dressing table stool for Anna. She knelt down next to her maid and brushed a lock of hair out of her eyes.

The girl's lip quivered, and finally, she said, so low Rosemary almost couldn't hear her, "I can't go with you to America."

Puzzled, Rosemary pressed, "But why are you crying? Who said you couldn't go? Constable Clayton?" If Anna's young groom-to-be had already begun flexing his authoritative muscles, Rosemary had half a mind to hunt him down and toss him forcefully into the river.

"Not him, no," Anna said with a vehement shake of her head. "It's my mum."

In all the time Anna had been in her employ, Rosemary could count on one hand the number of times she'd mentioned her family. It happened so rarely one could almost forget Anna had a mother of her own, that she didn't belong only to Rosemary.

"Is she afraid?" Rosemary asked, thinking of her own mother's reaction—one of concern for her and her brother's safety. One couldn't blame Evelyn, really; she'd already lost one child and couldn't bear the thought of losing another.

Anna's mouth flattened into a line. "Not in the way you mean. She's afraid if I leave, Morris's attention will wander. She says it's a miracle he wants me in the first place and I can't afford to leave him unattended; that I should press for a short engagement; that I don't have unlimited options like a—" Anna stopped short, looked guiltily into Rosemary's eyes but held her chin high, "like a rich girl. She says I'm not one, and I ought not to put on airs."

Rosemary bristled internally but kept her voice even. "Rich girl, poor girl, it makes no difference. People stray, and not just men, but I don't think you'd have agreed to marry Constable Clayton if you thought he would be unfaithful or harsh, if he were the type to write you off over a few weeks or even months apart. You've displayed good judgment, always. I trust it, as well should you."

Brows drawn together, Anna's head tilted to one side. Rosemary read the uncertainty there and continued, "My point, dear girl, is that it's your decision. Something tells me you'll get your chance to see America if it's something you truly desire; if you prefer to stay in London and plan your wedding, you have my blessing. However, it will be your choice and yours alone."

Anna considered and, after a few moments, finally seemed to decide. "I'm not afraid of losing Morris," she explained, "and I don't want to rush our engagement, but I also don't want to be away from him, not indefinitely."

"Then that's your answer, dear girl! Why, then, do you still look glum?" Rosemary asked when the clouds above Anna's head failed to retreat.

"It's just—how will you do without me on the ship? I'd be leaving you to your own devices; Miss Vera isn't even traveling with a maid. It wouldn't be right."

She managed not to laugh in Anna's face, but Rosemary couldn't help raising an eyebrow. "Darling girl, you need not worry about me. I shall find the strength to rally, and even if I find myself deep in the weeds, I'm sure the first-class stewarding staff will accommodate any request I might have. As for Miss Vera, she's managed in her own fashion for this long. I suspect she'll continue splendidly and only regret the absence of your company."

"Mum also said it was better to lose a post than a husband," Anna finally mumbled when Rosemary's words weren't enough to soothe her woes entirely.

"Well, she's not definitively wrong on that count, depending on the quality of the husband," Rosemary said wryly. "However, I've no intention of letting you go. My wardrobe, amongst other things, would be lost without you. Don't fret; you won't lose your post. We'll find something for you to do while I'm away. Perhaps a more thorough cleaning out of the attic or, if you'd prefer, you can help Jack tend the garden. If you don't mind traveling back with Max and Wadsworth, you can even tag along to see us off from Southampton tomorrow."

The reassurance finally broke through Anna's distraught countenance, and she loosed a tiny smile. "All right, Miss Rose. Thank you, truly," she said and got to work on the sorting with a bit more spring in her step.

Watching Anna take such care with her belongings, Rosemary made a decision. She'd make sure Wadsworth and the cook, Gladys, helped Anna plan a lovely little ceremony; they could have the reception in the back garden or even the park on the other side of the fence.

The girl deserved a special day and, indeed, a special life. Rosemary hoped Anna would be as happily married to Morris Clayton as she herself had been to Andrew. Sometimes, it felt to her as though that life had belonged to someone else. It stung, but the wound had finally scarred, and the sting lessened with each passing day.

Rosemary could never have that life again, but she could have a different one. Maybe, even one that didn't feel like a consolation prize.

Yes, kin or not, Anna deserved a special day, and Rosemary was determined to ensure it happened—once she returned from America. It wasn't one she'd miss for anything in the world.

Chapter Four

Wadsworth, Rosemary's butler (who wasn't any more thrilled by his mistress's travel plans than was her mother but kept his opinion to himself as butlers are expected to do), played chauffeur, arranging for the trip to Southampton and seeing to the luggage, which was no small feat given the number of trunks Vera insisted were necessary. Though Frederick had joked about the fact, there was a significant amount of truth behind his remarks.

Rosemary agreed with her brother; the voyage hardly seemed sufficiently lengthy to warrant such extensive effort. The crossing would take only five days each way, but Vera fussed over every outfit. She had planned her own and Frederick's ensembles down to the cuff links he would wear to dinner on their third evening at sea. They matched her earrings perfectly, by design, and the set had probably cost a fortune.

During the journey, Rosemary fretted over a niggling

worry that she had attempted to ignore. "Are you quite all right, Rose?" Max asked when she hadn't spoken for a solid ten minutes, during which time Frederick had regaled the car with a mind-numbingly technical description of the inner workings of steamship engines.

"My apologies," she said, giving Max's hand a squeeze. "It seems I'm rather more nervous about the journey than I realized. What if I'm positively miserable the entire time? I don't know how my stomach will fare," she explained.

Frederick boomed, "We're Woolridges; we've got stomachs of steel. You'll be just fine, Rosie, as will I." Rosemary wasn't sure which of them he was trying to convince, as neither had ever traveled aboard such a vessel. Their mother refused to step off dry land, and the closest they had come to a true ocean voyage was the ferry to the island of Cyprus. Rosemary recalled Anna's seasickness during the journey and took some comfort in knowing she herself had fared well on that occasion.

Vera brushed off the concern with a wave of her manicured fingers. "He's right, you know. I'm certain you'll be just fine. I'd be more concerned about your wardrobe." She had tried to impress upon Rosemary the importance of proper seafaring fashion but found her friend unmoved. Vera knew that, eventually, her friend would see the error of her ways.

As it turned out, eventually happened sooner than

even Vera had thought—before they'd stepped onto the ship, in fact! The unlikely Southampton docks backdropped a veritable fashion show befitting the pages of *Vogue* magazine. Though she wouldn't care to admit it aloud, Rosemary was grateful she'd allowed her friend to dress her for the launch.

Vera, naturally, looked quite comfortable and incredibly chic. She had chosen a sophisticated French ensemble. Designed to elicit scandal, the over-skirt was slit to flip open when she walked, revealing trousers of the same material underneath. The deep blue silk hadn't so much as wrinkled during the lengthy drive from London, and when Vera emerged from the car, the fabric fell into place, draping her figure at precisely the most flattering angle.

She had chosen a similar outfit—minus the trousers—for Rosemary, in a soft pink shade that perfectly set off her golden hair. A cropped jacket transformed her petite frame into something slightly more statuesque, an effect helped along by a pair of heels so high Rosemary felt as though she could see clear across the ocean.

Everywhere she looked, there was something interesting to see. People dressed in their best finery strolled along the quayside while workers scurried among them on a mission to complete the necessary work before it was time to depart.

Under the greasy smear of coal smoke, Rosemary

scented salty sea air. The pier seemed to go on forever, and then, there was the vessel itself. It was almost as if a skyscraper had been turned on its side and set afloat. Like soldiers in a row, three stacks towered over the top deck, smoke gently billowing out of their tops.

Max let out a low whistle while Anna's mouth dropped open at the sight. She had been quite content to accept Rosemary's offer to stay behind in London, but now that she was there, standing in front of such a masterpiece of shipbuilding, Anna appeared to doubt her decision. "It's quite impressive, isn't it?" she mused aloud.

"Indeed, a true feat of engineering," Frederick agreed, pointing to the ship's bow and explaining how it had been shaped to slice, as aerodynamically as possible, through the waves to create a smoother, faster travel experience for passengers. "They say if you avoid the upper decks, it's almost as though you aren't on a ship at all but inside a luxury hotel fit for the most sophisticated of travelers."

Anna nodded, absorbing every word, until Desmond commented, "Cunard ought to employ you to write the adverts, Freddie," and she nearly choked, attempting to suppress a giggle.

"You used to be my favorite, Anna," Frederick said, mock-seriously, then pointed towards the quayside. "Look, they're loading Vera's luggage now."

A large conveyor belt stretched from the edge of the quayside to a large opening in the ship's hull. What seemed to be a never-ending line of trunks and cases disappeared inside. Rosemary could only imagine the hubbub of activity happening below decks; what a feat it must be to sort and deliver it all!

Vera ignored her husband's sarcastic comment and confirmed with Wadsworth that her actual luggage was properly labeled. She needn't have worried. Her taupe trunks and cases, each with a stripe of navy, scarlet, and white down the center, were stacked like a pyramid in the back of the hired lorry, next to Rosemary's much smaller pile of luggage striped with cream and maroon.

"Miss Vera, do not fear," Wadsworth intoned, "it's all been organized with the utmost care. Each piece is color-coordinated and labeled either 'stateroom' or 'cargo'. I've been assured that the stewards are quite vigilant."

Just then, one of the vigilant stewards appeared. Impeccably turned out in his dark uniform suit with brass buttons, a lapel pin with the ship's insignia, stripes on the sleeves, and hat with another insignia worked in just above the brim, he had a competent air.

"He's correct, madam," the steward said. "Cunard prides itself on customer satisfaction, and every staff member is held to the highest standard. It's rare for anything to go missing. My name is Stratford, and please rest assured I'll personally look after your baggage."

Vera nodded, appeased, while Stratford checked their tickets, but added, "Pay special attention to the garment bag; it's couture." Indeed, the dress inside had been quite expensive and Vera had planned to save it for the final evening of festivities before arriving in New York.

"Of course, madam, it will be done," Stratford replied politely. "Now, if you'll all visit the purser and then submit to a brief inspection, you can begin boarding shortly. In fact, there's another passenger from your bank of staterooms checking in now—a Miss McCoy, who will be staying in the room directly across from yours, Mrs. Lillywhite."

The group headed in the direction Stratford had indicated to a booth where a robust, middle-aged lady wearing a brightly patterned shawl on top of a lace dress towered over the purser. A large silk flower pinned just below her neckline flapped in the pungent sea breeze.

"Nonsense! There must be something you can do," she insisted. Next to her, a slight man in his mid-30s with almost translucent skin appeared embarrassed. He carried a jacket and a spiral notebook in one arm and a small suitcase in the other, and it took him a moment to catch his breath.

"I'll take a berth in second class," he said, "or even third. I'm sure there's a ticket to be had, isn't that right?"

The purser nodded his head. "My sincere apologies, Miss McCoy, but your secretary will need to go round to the ticket office," he explained and pointed out directions. "It's all the way on the other side of the docks. You'll want to hurry."

"It's preposterous," the huffy Miss McCoy continued to rant, her eyes frosty beneath a layer of her thick fringe. "We booked two first-class staterooms. Mr. Sutton has asthma. It's quite serious, and his doctor has insisted upon fresh air. I won't have him languishing in third class." Suddenly, she seemed far less of a pill and more a concerned employer. "There must be something you can do," she continued to press.

Instead of softening, the purser turned grim. "Do you mean to tell me this man is in ill health? Our health standards are strict for good reason: to protect the other passengers."

At that, Mr. Sutton drew up to his full height and suddenly didn't appear quite so inconsequential. "It's asthma; I was born with it, and it's not contagious. Furthermore, my doctor, the finest in London, has cleared me for travel."

The purser was unmoved. "Tell that to the inspector, but first, you'll need a ticket."

Rosemary made a quick, easy decision and stepped forward. "Excuse me, but perhaps I can help. Our party was reduced at the last moment; I have an extra ticket for a berth in first-class. I believe it's just diagonally opposite from your stateroom."

The lady perked her head up, appraised Rosemary with appreciation, and offered her hand, "I'm Trix McCoy, and I would be in your debt. Mr. Sutton is essential to my work."

"Rosemary Lillywhite," she replied. "Pleased to meet you."

From the depths of her memory, Rosemary dredged up the name, realizing after a moment that Trix McCoy was the author of the bestselling book in Britain: *Mrs. Willoughby and the Poisoned Pen.* Murder mysteries weren't Rosemary's genre of choice, at least not since she'd begun solving them in real life, but the author's success was impressive, and Rosemary found herself intrigued.

"It's no trouble, really. My lady's maid got engaged, and well, she decided not to come along with me after all," Rosemary explained.

Miss McCoy nodded and said with a trace of impatience, "I'm eager to hear the whole tale once we're settled in—perhaps later, at dinner? We'll be neighbors, won't we, for the next five days; I'm certain we'll all become quite well acquainted."

She spared a short nod for Rosemary's traveling companions, and with that, Rosemary surrendered her ticket and accepted Mr. Sutton's gracious thanks. The purser observed the exchange impassively and waved them all through to the examination booth, where they were each asked a short series of health-related questions before being cleared for boarding.

During the process, another group of passengers—consisting of a young lady with a pretty but nondescript face, an older gentleman wearing a tweed jacket, and a couple, the female half of which was carrying an expensive French handbag as fashionable as anything in Vera's wardrobe—approached the booth, and Rosemary overheard enough of the purser's comments to deduce they would be traveling in the compartment adjacent to Rosemary's own.

Then, Stratford distributed the party's boarding materials. "Here are the keys to your staterooms, a ship map, and of course, your first-class passenger and staff list. Please make yourselves familiar with, and confine yourselves to, the areas marked as suitable for your class designation. We make these distinctions for the comfort and safety of all classes of passengers."

Frederick accepted the proffered lists, scanned the passenger sheet hastily, then handed it to Vera. "This is more in your line of things, Vera dear. I wouldn't recognize a single luminary."

"She'll have had tea with half of them," Desmond agreed with a snort, causing Vera to resolutely tuck the list in with the rest of her things and pretend not to have heard him.

Mr. Sutton accepted his items and placed the paperwork inside the cover of the spiral notebook, but before he could get it tucked back into the crook of his arm, a young boy from the other group of passengers knocked into his arm and sent it tumbling to the ground.

"Sorry," the lad mumbled, hurrying along behind his family without a backward glance.

With a smile Mr. Sutton waved a hand. "Boys will be boys, but we can't lose that, can we, Trix?" he asked loudly enough to be overheard by everyone in the vicinity. "That's our next bestseller."

The author managed to look pleased without actually smiling but didn't have time to comment since Stratford had introduced a second steward who would show her and her companion to their staterooms.

When that task was done, Stratford turned back to Rosemary's group.

"Your trunks will be distributed as per your man's detailed instructions," he explained while he walked, nodding to Wadsworth. "Luggage designated for your stateroom will be delivered while you enjoy drinks and a departure celebration in the first-class Observation Lounge bar. First, however, I'll show you to your accommodation."

With Wadsworth and Anna trailing behind and

Stratford leading the way, Rosemary followed her friends—old and new—up the ramp and onto the ship.

CHAPTER FIVE

"You're standing on the Promenade Deck now," Stratford explained once they'd crossed the ramp and been deposited one level below the topmost deck. "This is the first-class entrance, and as you can see, if you peer down over the railing, it encompasses four levels, all the way down to the Grand Saloon where you'll gather for dinner each night."

He said it so nonchalantly that someone with poor eyesight would never be able to tell there was anything to lament missing, but Rosemary was mesmerized. Max squeezed her hand and gazed around appreciatively at the entrance's decorative elements, done in the modern style.

No fussy, frescoed ceilings : just endless sections of elegant but understated tray ceiling. A series of columns marched down either side of the room, their fluted pattern repeated in the raised wall panels with accents of green and silver trim. Between the columns, gleaming

31

fan-shaped sconces wrought from metal and glass cast interesting shadows across the diamond-patterned floor. Before she could hold it back, Rosemary let out a sigh.

Stratford stopped, turned, and pointed. "Here, you have the shops and the private Millionaires' Suites beyond; aft is the Observation Lounge bar—that's where you'll go for late-night drinks and dancing—and the smoking rooms; and of course, running along the perimeter, is the open-air promenade, for strolls and a view of the waves."

He reiterated the ship's strict policy regarding class distinction, though he made it sound less like a warning and more like a promise that their group wouldn't have to fret over lower-class passengers wandering into their section.

"The shuffleboard courts and gym are on the Boat Deck above, and my advice is to enjoy your time in the fresh air. We'll be heading into colder waters before you can blink. Ladies and gentleman, please follow me," he said and approached the lifts.

"Your staterooms are just one floor down on the B Deck. The purser and steward services are on Deck C with the laundry and beauty salons. Deck D is the aforementioned dining saloon; E is mostly staff accommodations, and F is where you'll find the pool and Turkish baths. It's not as complicated as it seems; if it's your first time with us, please don't fret. There are ship directories[1] on every level."

Trix McCoy stopped short of the lifts and declined to enter. "I'll just meet you down there," she said, backing away. "I prefer to use the stairs." Her secretary remained in the lift, his placid expression indicating her decision was nothing out of the ordinary.

"Very well, madam," the steward said and nodded to the operator. "Here we are," he announced when the lift stopped on their floor a few moments later. Miss McCoy reached the bottom of the stairs by the time the luggage had been emptied, just in time to step back in next to Mr. Sutton.

"The Winter Garden Lounge is down that way. I recommend it for afternoon tea or if you enjoy ferns," Stratford said, pointing aft as he walked quickly in the opposite direction. Rosemary's compartment— compartment B2C—wasn't far from the lift—through a set of baize doors and then a sharp left just across from the stewardess station. From there, the compartment branched into two sections. The other group of passengers was similarly gathered in the foremost one, listening to a nearly identical lecture from a nearly identical steward.

"And here are your staterooms," Stratford said finally. "Miss McCoy is first on the interior side, followed by Mr. Cooper; Mrs. Lillywhite, you're to the right, with

---

[1] For a deck plan visit www.emilyqueenwriter.com/deck-plan

Mr. Sutton beyond. In the end, in a lovely double suite, Mr. and Mrs. Woolridge. You'll find our amenities are top-notch, and of course, if you gentlemen need anything, I'll be your personal steward for the duration of your voyage. The ladies will have Molly, and rest assured, she's more than competent."

"It's quite all right, Trix," Rosemary heard Mr. Sutton say quietly, his voice a plea. "Beggars can't be choosers."

The author waved away the comment. "Nonsense, what's the harm?" she replied and then turned to Rosemary and asked sweetly, "You wouldn't perhaps mind switching to the stateroom on the other side of the hall, would you? That way, you would be next to your traveling companion and I'd be next to mine."

It was a simple enough request, and it did make sense, so Rosemary agreed without making any sort of a fuss. Still, the exchange let her know much about the author. She and Max shared a glance of impatience and were grateful when Stratford promised to send the aforementioned Molly to Miss McCoy's room straight away, and the hallway finally cleared.

More than a mere cabin, Rosemary's stateroom consisted of three separate areas: a sitting room with a desk and chair, a bedroom, and a private lavatory. There was more than enough space to spread out, to her delight.

"Perhaps I made the correct decision," Anna murmured quietly as she said her goodbyes. "I'd get lost on a ship this large and forget where to find my berth!"

Rosemary winked and kissed the girl's cheek. "You'd find your sea legs, I've no doubt," she said, even though she felt quite overwhelmed herself after the steward's whirlwind tour. "Goodbye, dear girl. Goodbye, Wadsworth," she said, knowing better than to attempt any display of affection towards her reserved butler.

He cleared his throat and bade her goodbye, nearly cracking a smile when Vera called, "Don't throw any wild parties while we're away!"

Max assured Wadsworth he'd join him and Anna back on the quayside, and he and Rosemary were finally allowed a few private moments.

"Suddenly, I'm having second thoughts," she said into Max's shirt sleeve as he wrapped her in his arms for one last embrace. She looked up at him and made a final plea. "You could just remain on board; I'm sure they wouldn't notice one little stowaway!"

Max sighed, said, "If anyone could convince me, it would be you," and looked into her eyes. "Rosemary—"

Whatever Max had intended to say was interrupted by the sound of a steward hollering, "All ashore that's going to shore!" several times while banging a cowbell.

"I suppose I ought to be off," Max said instead, the moment ruined.

Disappointed, Rosemary nodded and followed him out of the stateroom, where they met Vera, Frederick, and Desmond and headed back up to the Promenade Deck.

"So long, Rosemary Lillywhite," Max said sadly before disembarking. She couldn't find the words to reply, and she didn't want to cry, so she watched his retreating back until he disappeared into the crowd on the other side of the ramp. She spotted Anna and Wadsworth, and before long, Max joined them, and then it was the rumble of engines and the roar of the ship's horn.

The crowd erupted as the ship began to move, pulling away from the quayside slowly but quickly picking up speed, and though Rosemary couldn't hear over the din, she could imagine the sound of a thousand poppers as a rainbow of streamers exploded into the air.

Max touched his fingers to his lips and raised them in the air, throwing a kiss out onto the sea. Rosemary wished she could reach out and grab it, hold on to it for the length of the journey. Her heart constricted painfully as the ship pulled away from the quayside, and the distance between them increased. While she watched, Max began to blend into the crowd, and when he was merely a dot in a wash of other dots, Rosemary turned away and dried her tears. Whatever happened with Max, she was determined to enjoy herself.

Rosemary's mood brightened further when she rejoined her friends. The promenade was less crowded now that the quayside had nearly disappeared—and she had yet to feel anything resembling seasickness!

Many of the passengers had retreated to the Observation Lounge bar, choosing instead to enjoy the view of the sea away from the sun and salty air. Rosemary wanted to press her face to the glass like her young nephew, Nelly, would have been sure to do and gape at the wonders on the other side. Stratford had mentioned dancing, but it was still only afternoon, and the atmosphere resembled a pub's. She could see cards being dealt at a few of the tables and cocktails being poured at the bar.

"Let's have a walkabout before it's time to dress for dinner," Vera suggested, linking arms with Rosemary and steering her back in the direction of the first-class entrance.

"Let's go this way." Frederick took Vera's free arm and deftly steered them both away from the shops and towards the lift. Vera let him, but with a smug smile and a wink in Rosemary's direction that clearly said "all in good time" and "what Frederick doesn't know won't kill him." Poor Freddie, Rosemary thought and then decided he'd make do, somehow, without her pity.

Any thought of shopping went straight out of Vera's head anyway when her attention was caught by someone—or rather, two someones—coming through from the promenade on the opposite side of the ship.

Vera's fingernails dug into flesh, causing Frederick to curse and Rosemary to yank her arm away. Holding on even tighter, Vera squeaked, "Do you know who that is?"

When her gaze followed Vera's and she realized what all the fuss was about, Rosemary's eyebrows shot towards her hairline. It took a great deal of effort to rearrange her face into a neutral expression, but she managed to do so and retorted, "Of course I do, you dolt. I don't live under a stone, do I?"

For sauntering their way across the tile-patterned floor were Gianni and Mirella Verratti, the famous Italian singing duo that had taken the world by storm with their impossible talent and stunning good looks. One couldn't visit a single nightclub in London without hearing a rendition of at least one Verratti duet.

The whole of Britain had gone crazy for the couple; everyone knew who they were, and the papers followed their every move. Had the fuss only been for their music, the attention would have been understandable; the Verrattis possessed talent in scores. However, it was more than that that made them stars—it was the way they seemed to adore one another. Mr. Verratti looked at his wife the way any woman wanted her husband to look at her—as if he had eyes only for her!

It couldn't have been difficult; Mirella Verratti was the epitome of everything a modern woman was supposed to be. Together, she and Gianni made the perfect golden couple.

For instance, Mrs. Verratti wore an outfit resembling those of the more fashion-conscious first-class passengers: a silk suit not dissimilar to those Rosemary and Vera both sported. Except, the stitching featured greater detail, and the high waist nipped inwards at a slightly more stylish angle.

She appeared at once out of place (indeed, where did such a creature belong?) and also entirely at home both onboard and in her buffed-to-a-golden-glow skin. At her elbow draped a man so astonishingly attractive he was almost ugly, though until she'd seen his photograph, Rosemary hadn't realized such a thing could be possible. The effect was even more pronounced in person.

He stood, head tilted, the fingers of one hand tapping against his leg while his wife graciously autographed passenger lists for the few brave souls who dared make an approach. Behind the couple, on the promenade, a handful of hopeful gawkers unabashedly gaped through the glass at the singer.

"That's her singing partner and husband," Vera explained.

Again, Rosemary rolled her eyes. "I know."

"He's been called the best-dressed man in all the

magazines and society papers."

Rosemary could understand why; Mr. Verratti had as much class as his companion. It practically rolled out of his ears. And yet, Frederick sniffed, and Desmond snorted.

"Would either of you like to borrow my lace handkerchief?" Rosemary asked sharply.

"No, but he probably would. He looks like a zebra escaped from the zoo. You can't deny it," Frederick said in his and Desmond's defense.

Vera dug her fingernails into Frederick's arm again, sharper this time, and his mouth shut with a snap.

Yes, Mr. Verratti's outfit was slightly louder and perhaps even a bit snugger than what a Brit might choose, but he wasn't British, was he? Of course, despite rumblings about being ever so cultured and sophisticated, Frederick and Desmond were quite conservative when it came to personal style. Rosemary couldn't remember her brother ever sporting a different haircut, even as a boy. His attitude chafed, and she hoped he wouldn't be a pill for the entire trip.

The celebrity couple spent a few minutes being photographed by a man who Rosemary took for a journalist, for when he had finished, he let the camera hang around his neck on a strap and retrieved a pad and pencil from his coat pocket. After talking with him for a spell, during which he took copious notes, the couple was finally able to break free. Despite the hubbub, when she approached the lift, Mrs. Verratti's lips were curled into an easy smile.

She nodded at each of the people waiting to board, dazzling Frederick and Desmond and rendering Vera positively speechless. "What a lovely headpiece," the singer said to Vera, her smile a veritable beam of sunlight, her voice a musical lilt.

Instead of responding, Vera simply stared for a few awkward moments until Rosemary answered in her place. "Thank you, Mrs. Verratti. My friend Vera here has excellent taste—and she's a big fan of yours—both of you, of course," Rosemary added when words continued to escape her usually effusive friend. Mr. Verratti merely smiled placidly, as though the experience of his wife being fawned over was a daily occurrence to be endured rather than enjoyed. Perhaps, Rosemary realized, for him, it was.

"*Molte grazie*." the vision in violet replied graciously, as though the compliment hadn't been delivered in rather an odd, awkward manner. "I do hope our performance on the eve of our arrival will live up to your expectations," she added.

"Oh, I'm sure there won't be any trouble there," Desmond piped up, just grateful to be looked upon by the beautiful singer, even for a moment.

When the lift arrived, the group stepped back and

waved for Mrs. Verratti and her husband to claim it. In a higher-than-normal pitch, Frederick assured, "We'll take the next one."

As soon as the Verrattis were gone, Vera's voice returned. "Good grief! I'm not sure there's a way I could have looked more like a complete idiot!" she wailed.

Desmond couldn't seem to help himself. "Actually, you could have—" Vera cut him off with a glare, and he gave her a wide berth before continuing from a safe distance, "I told you to check the passenger list the purser gave you. Had you heeded my advice, you would have known the names of all the notable guests."

Looking as though she'd quite rather swim back to shore than admit Desmond was right, Vera's mouth snapped closed once more.

Chapter Six

"Come on, old chap." Frederick clapped Desmond on the shoulder when Vera began readying herself two hours before dinner. "Unless you wish to be exposed to a debate on the merits of chiffon over wash satin, you'd better make your escape with me."

"For your information," Vera began, but with a mischievous smile tossed back over his shoulder, Frederick was already at the door, Desmond hard on his heels. "Be back in time to escort us to dinner. If you're late . . ." She let the threat trail off, but the implications were ominous.

"We shall return anon." Desmond bowed as if in the presence of royalty and then scampered away when Vera growled at him.

The men took themselves off to begin making trouble, leaving Rosemary (who would quite rather have gone along with them) behind.

It being night one, she was more than happy to

appease her friend by dressing up, but Rosemary had no intention of indulging Vera every evening of the journey! Still, she spent the requisite time attending to her hair and makeup, determined to make herself equal to the gorgeous gown she had selected for the occasion.

Even though she hadn't rushed, Rosemary finished with forty-five minutes to spare. The seasickness she had fretted over still had not arrived, and she was beginning to think perhaps she was out of the woods after all. A steel Woolridge stomach, as Frederick had predicted.

Now that she'd thought of her stomach, it began to rumble, and Rosemary realized she was absolutely ravenous. Dinner couldn't come soon enough, and the last thing she wanted to do was spend nearly an hour thinking about food. Instead, she decided to spend the extra time taking a peek at the library situated just aft of the Winter Garden Lounge.

Rosemary took one last look in the mirror, touched up her lipstick, and after one last preparation, ducked out of her stateroom. Molly, the stewardess, was just closing Trix McCoy's door, and she pasted a smile on her face Rosemary immediately recognized as artifice. Vera nodded sympathetically, but the stewardess's veneer didn't so much as crack as she pushed her trolley past the two women. Seasoned were the first-class staff, Rosemary quickly surmised.

In the common area between the two banks of suites, two little girls aged approximately two and seven played while an older lad—perhaps twelve or thirteen and evidently a brother—leafed through a comic. Every time the youngest girl tried to stand up on shaky feet, the boy would say sharply and without tearing his eyes from the page, "No, Franny," and the older girl would patiently pull the toddler back onto her bottom.

Then, the baby would let out a peal of laughter that elicited a smile from an otherwise churlish-looking gentleman seated nearby. Rosemary recognized him as the one wearing the tweed jacket when they'd embarked earlier.

"Hello there," the man said, perking up immediately at the sight of Rosemary. His eyes raked her up and down, though in the benevolent way a grandfather might appraise his granddaughter. Except, despite a thick beard of white, this man didn't look quite old enough for that. "You must be half of the couple in the large suite, eh?" he more suggested than asked.

Rosemary excused his presumption, but the concept struck her funny, most likely due to the brandy she'd impulsively downed just before exiting her stateroom, which had landed more heavily than anticipated on her empty stomach. "No, actually, but the man is my brother, and we're traveling together."

"So you won't be needing an escort to dinner, then?"

the man asked hopefully. "I'd be the envy of the Grand Saloon with you on my arm. It would be a coup for an old relic such as myself."

"You don't look so old to me," Rosemary heard herself toss back cheekily.

"Beautiful and kindhearted," he replied. "A deadly combination. I'm Dennis Tait, by the way. And you are?"

Rosemary offered her hand. "Rosemary Lillywhite," she replied. "Pleased to meet you."

"Miss Lillywhite," said Mr. Tait, and Rosemary corrected him reflexively. "I beg your pardon, Mrs. Lillywhite," he revised. "I shall apologize to your husband," he winked now, "and inform him he's a lucky man, though I suspect I won't be the first to make the same observation."

The comment sucked the breath out of her, but Rosemary smiled anyway. "I'm a widow, actually."

Mr. Tait's brows drew together. "We have something in common then. Please, accept my apologies."

"Please don't worry about it, truly, and I won't hold it against you," she assured and declined the kind invitation. "I've been promised to another this evening, but surely I'll see you at dinner? Perhaps we can have a chat?"

"I'll hold you to that, Mrs. Lillywhite," he replied with a wink. As she headed down the corridor towards the library, Rosemary heard him say to the young boy, "That's how you do it, young chap," and couldn't help but smile.

So far, life on board ship was going swimmingly, Rosemary thought, pardoning herself the unintended pun.

CHAPTER SEVEN

Dinner was to be served at eight in the Grand Saloon, located two levels down on D Deck, at the bottom of the impressive grand staircase. Surrounded by comfortable-looking shell-backed chairs upholstered in plush velvet, polished tables occupied the dining hall on one side, while a sumptuous lounge and reception room spread across the other.

Of course, Rosemary had heard tell of the *grand descent*, where all the notable first-class passengers would arrive dressed in their most fashionable outfits and descend the stairs to the dining hall in dramatic fashion. She simply hadn't expected ever to do it herself, nor had she known just how many stairs she would be required to navigate wearing high-heeled shoes.

"You look lovely," Desmond said as he appraised the vision before him. Georgian crepe in blue so dark it was almost black swept along Rosemary's curves all the way down to her hips, then flared out to gently swish around her feet.

Desmond acted as the perfect gentleman, and even though she didn't slip, it was nice to know that he was there to catch her. If only she wasn't still wishing it were Max at her side!

Like many of the others, Vera had prepared herself with the same gusto she would any other performance. Indeed, that was how she viewed it, much as she did the rest of life—as if the world were merely a stage set and dressed expressly for her.

Of course, she always stole the show and therefore had been given no reason to assume her attitude was based in anything other than reality. It was a trait Rosemary both adored and envied, yet which also frustrated her frequently and at great length.

Rosemary wondered what it might be like to be so carefree, to worry only about oneself rather than fret over the feelings of others. Of course, Vera did care underneath it all, and on more than one occasion, Rosemary had watched her lament her own shortcomings.

Later, for instance, Vera would be compelled to apologize to Frederick for taking him to task over his dinner ensemble, having realized she'd acted like a troll to her husband, who had only wanted to show off his new cravat. It wasn't his fault he didn't understand that its pattern clashed with her beautiful dress!

Frederick escorted his wife down the stairs, wearing the face he had been trained to display from birth—one of good breeding, class, and decorum. It was a rare sight, indeed, but Vera appeared grateful, though truly he hadn't fooled her in the least. He was only behaving now to give himself an excuse to misbehave later.

At the bottom, the foursome caught sight of Miss McCoy and Mr. Sutton. She wore another eccentric outfit, and Mr. Sutton's complexion appeared alabaster against the black of his suit. In good spirits, Miss McCoy offered, "Our table is just there," and pointed to a prime location with an excellent view of the staircase, "if you'd care to join us."

Once settled, Rosemary caught sight of the group from the other half of the B Deck compartment two tables to the right and waved to Mr. Tait. She was caught somewhat off guard when the companion of the lady with the fashionable handbag waved back at her instead. It took another moment for her to realize that he'd been waving to Frederick.

"Someone you know?" she asked her brother.

"Not really. It's a chap from the other half of our compartment—Mr. Parsons, and that's his wife," Frederick explained. "We met him in the lounge."

Going turncoat, Desmond sold his friend out. "Yeah, and he lightened your wallet, didn't he, Freddie?"

"As if you've never lost a bet," Frederick replied

sourly.

Vera gazed at her husband curiously, but before she could ask what he'd been up to, something else caught her attention across the room.

Desmond's eyes swept up over the top of Rosemary's head and went misty as he, too, trailed off and stared, his mouth going slack for a moment before he swallowed hard. Rosemary turned around and realized, quite quickly, the reason for her friends' distraction.

Mirella Verratti, even more stunning than she had been some hours earlier, if it were possible, posed at the top of the stairs—a perfect hourglass silhouette that wouldn't have been out of place on the pages of a magazine or in a Parisian fashion parade. Rosemary suddenly felt like a duck in a swan pond, entirely plain by comparison. It seemed Vera felt the same; her eyes narrowed infinitesimally for a moment that none but her traveling companions would notice before her face smoothed back into its previous placid veneer.

The singer stopped, stood for a few long moments, and looked around as if ensuring she had captured the attention of the entire saloon before beginning her descent. At her side, wearing an enigmatic expression, stood Mr. Verratti, whose pinstriped suit was indisputably nautical but nevertheless entirely inappropriate for dinner.

In fact, the room was abuzz, and even Desmond

appeared incredulous, his lips turned down into a frown. When he noted the inquisitive expressions on his companions' faces, Desmond explained, "It's just not done. He's got mettle; I'll give him that."

Amused, Rosemary realized Mr. Verratti's eyebrow was raised not in consternation but rather as a challenge to anyone who dared to shame him for eschewing the traditional solid black.

He held on to his love's arm, stopping to gaze at her admiringly when they reached the landing between two banks of stairs, and eliciting a murmur of approval from the crowd. She, in turn, leaned her head in his direction, basking in the warmth of his gaze.

Vera looked on with soft eyes; Desmond, on the other hand, made a crude retching sound just loud enough for his friends to hear. Rosemary shot him a quelling look and wondered how someone so concerned with proper dinner attire could be so crass.

Stiffening her resolve not to think any more about Max and romance, Rosemary agreed with the sentiment, if not Desmond's delivery. "That was so sickly I think I'll have to cry off when they bring round the dessert trolley," she said under her breath. "There's only so much sugar I can stomach."

Her ears keen even when her eyes were elsewhere, Vera turned her attention away from the public display of affection and looked over to ask, "When did you become such a cynic, Rosie?"

Trix McCoy laughed loudly and said, "Better a cynic than a peasant. So often, these celebrities pant for attention in the most unbecoming fashion, and usually, their entire image is nothing more than a facade. If you ask me, people who lie for a living ought not to be trusted."

"I don't recall anyone *having* asked you," Vera replied icily, taking great offense at the comment. Miss McCoy's lip twitched, but she maintained her composure.

Desmond, his glass now empty, guffawed. "You inadvertently stepped into the lion's den with that comment, I'm afraid, Miss McCoy. Vera here is an actress, you see, and since lying essentially comes with the territory, she's understandably concerned about her reputation."

"It's quite all right," Miss McCoy replied, even though Desmond hadn't exactly apologized, and Vera certainly had no intention of doing so.

"You're an author, aren't you?" Vera asked but didn't wait for an answer before adding, "Of murder mysteries, I believe. Fiction, I presume, unless you're a stickler for accurate research. Either way, what you do is not all that different from what I do, in the end. We both tell stories, ones that aren't entirely truthful."

Vera's remark appeared to put Trix McCoy in her

place, and the author suddenly became preoccupied with her menu. She squinted at the fine print and then set it back down, the expression on her face giving Rosemary the impression she hadn't been able to make out a word.

Later, after the first course had been served, Mr. Sutton—Dolph, as he'd insisted upon being called—flushed when he caught Rosemary's eye and she smiled, but he managed to ask in a clear, steady voice, "Is this your first time on a transatlantic liner?"

"Yes, it is," Rosemary replied, grateful for the change of subject. "And far overdue."

"So you're enjoying yourself, then. You're not bothered by the motion?"

"No, not at all. Is that so hard to believe?" she asked when his lips turned down into a dubious expression. Despite his vaguely sickly appearance, Dolph wasn't an unattractive man; he was intelligent and had kind chestnut-colored eyes and an easy smile.

He shook his head. "No, not at all. I'm simply envious. The ship does not agree with my ailments, and the journey can be quite miserable without the right medication and ministrations—strong ginger tea, fresh air, an attentive steward. It's all very tiresome, indeed. Nothing a lady would care to discuss over dinner."

"I'm sorry it's so unpleasant for you," Rosemary said, waving off the comment. The pair chatted amicably throughout the meal, the kind of companionable conversation that skirted any controversial topics such as politics or religion.

She inquired as to whether he enjoyed his job as secretary to Miss McCoy, genuinely curious what it might be like for two people who seemed like opposites to work together day in and day out.

"It's work; there are ups and downs, of course," Dolph explained, "but she's much more understanding than most employers these days and far less demanding. Most importantly, even if it does sometimes take her a while to ask for help, she's intelligent enough to know she doesn't know everything. It's a rare quality, that."

Rosemary wholeheartedly agreed and looked upon Miss McCoy with even more interest. She was an enigma: mildly abrasive yet highly regarded. An interesting juxtaposition, to be certain.

When the last course had been cleared, and the music switched to something more upbeat, Frederick asked Vera to dance, and they took to the floor. "Care to join them?" Desmond asked Rosemary.

"Not just yet," she said, declining the invitation. "I shouldn't have gone for dessert after all; I feel like a stuffed pig."

Desmond placed a hand on his own stomach. "I second that," he replied, just as Rosemary looked up to see Mr. Tait from the common room approaching the dining table.

He smiled as if she were an old friend, and poor Dolph's face fell as her attention was further diluted.

"Ah, Mrs. Lillywhite, we meet again, and once more, the pleasure is mine," he said, earning himself a dubious look from Desmond, who, upon inspection, evidently didn't see any reason to concern himself with Rosemary's honor and settled back into his chair.

"It was lovely to have talked to you, Mrs. Lillywhite," Dolph said then, rising from his chair and gathering his jacket, "but I think I'd better go back to my suite and lie down. Good evening."

"Did I scare the gentleman off?" Mr. Tait asked, watching Dolph's retreating back curiously.

Rosemary laughed. "I think rather you might have," she replied and then said to Miss McCoy, "Although, I suspect he retreated for the benefit of his health. I certainly hope he's going to be all right."

Miss McCoy waved a hand. "He has the latest inhaler, and the best medicines money can buy. Most likely, he's gone off to pore over the notes I made on the journey to the docks. My penmanship is indecipherable on the best of days."

"Dolph is Miss McCoy's secretary," Rosemary explained to Mr. Tait. "Perhaps you've read her book, *Mrs. Willoughby and the Poisoned Pen*. It's quite a sensation," she gushed in an attempt to appease her neighbor following Vera's impolite remarks.

Mr. Tait's eyes flicked back and forth as he racked his brain for the book's name. "No, I'm sorry, I haven't heard of it," he apologized.

Miss McCoy's eyes flashed, but she offered graciously, "I've got extra copies in my stateroom should you wish to give it a read." Indeed, Rosemary wouldn't have been surprised to discover the lady had trunks full of her own books stashed away below decks.

Mr. Tait merely nodded thinly, as though murder mysteries—particularly one featuring an intrepid female sleuth as the reviews loved to quote—might not be his cup of tea. He turned his attention back to Rosemary when she asked, mercifully, "So, are you traveling for business or pleasure?"

"For pleasure, of course," Mr. Tait replied, "I'm a man of some leisure," he explained, "and I find all forms of travel stimulating. Observing people is something of a hobby of mine. I'm an observer of life, you could say. And you, I assume this is a pleasure cruise for you as well—unless you're one of those modern women with her own empire?"

Rosemary laughed, and they continued to chat for a few moments until Vera and Frederick returned from the dance floor. "You'll never believe it, Rosie," Vera gushed, "but I eavesdropped on Mirella Verratti, and then I did a bit of pressing and managed to secure us a shuffleboard court right next to hers tomorrow afternoon on the Boat Deck!"

Suddenly, and before Rosemary could reply to Vera's exuberant statement, the ship hit rough waters and lurched sharply enough she could feel her stomach roll. All the blood drained from her face, and when she looked up at her brother, she realized she wasn't the only one who had been affected.

"Oh no," she exclaimed, clapping a hand over her mouth. Frederick looked positively green, and when another swell caused Rosemary's stomach to flip over again, she decided perhaps the Woolridge constitution wasn't as hardy as she'd originally thought.

"I think, my dear," said Mr. Tait, "you had better forgo the remainder of the festivities. Get back to your stateroom, post-haste—both of you." He nodded at Rosemary and also Frederick, who appeared relieved, while Vera looked crestfallen.

"Don't you worry, old chap." Desmond clapped Frederick on the back. "I'll take care of your wife and deliver her back to your suite after we've had a cocktail—or perhaps two."

A very short discussion ensued where Frederick agreed Vera should stay with Desmond and have a grand time. There was no reason why she ought to miss the festivities. "I'd prefer you didn't see me like this anyway, dear," Frederick insisted when she attempted a weak protest.

Mr. Tait stood and looked between Rosemary and Frederick. "It's high time I retired to my own room, as well. Would you like to share the lift?"

"Why not," Frederick agreed, "as long as you aren't averse to the possibility of seeing my dinner in reverse."

"Freddie, kindly put a lid on it, won't you?" Rosemary chided her brother before kissing Vera on the cheek and following Mr. Tait to the lift.

CHAPTER EIGHT

Mr. Tait had been correct about the importance of a good stewardess; Rosemary didn't know what she might have done without Molly, who reminded her of her butler, Wadsworth, exemplifying an efficiency often mistaken for compassion—the latter only a light lining to the former.

The girl had even procured a copy of the ship's newspaper, *The Atlantic Edition* which, given they'd only departed the previous evening, was mostly adverts and stock prices, with a long article about the Verratti couple and their anticipated performance. Still, it felt quite modern to read a paper printed right on board the ship! With fewer than 600 available and over two thousand passengers on board, one couldn't be guaranteed a copy. Rosemary tucked hers into her handbag to keep as a souvenir.

Though she hadn't got much rest, her stomach had settled overnight, and by the time she awoke, she was positively ravenous. She found her sea legs and tore through the luggage delivered to her room the previous evening, searching for one of the outfits Vera had promised would be appropriate for daytime at sea. Yet, the suitcase filled with crepe de Chine sport dresses was nowhere to be found.

Thinking perhaps the bag had ended up in one of her companions' suites by mistake, Rosemary chose another outfit. Her concern, at that moment, was quieting her rumbling stomach, not impressing the other passengers with her fashion sense.

Surprisingly, she found Vera, her brother, and Desmond in the dining saloon; unsurprisingly, she recognized the signs that Vera and Desmond—along with a large portion of the room—battled the heavy-headed beast of the dreaded hangover. Frederick, however, had taken kindly to the steward's ministrations and looked significantly fresher, if still a bit pale.

He sat next to the young boy Rosemary remembered from the common room and engaged in lively conversation while Vera focused on drinking her tea in tiny little sips. Whatever she and Desmond had gotten up to the night before, they both looked the worse for wear.

"Good morning," Rosemary said, taking the chair next to Vera and receiving a pair of grunts in reply. "You'll feel better once you've put something greasy into your stomach," Rosemary assured, feeling sanctimonious even though she probably would have been in the same boat had she not been forced to retire early the previous evening.

When neither Desmond nor Vera engaged in conversation, she turned her attention to the couple she assumed to be the parents of the two young girls and the boy chatting to Frederick.

"We're visiting my husband's family in the States," Mrs. Lois Long explained after introducing herself and her husband, Alaric.

She didn't give Rosemary time to reply or even state her name but chattered on loudly. "They live in Rhode Island, and they're incredibly wealthy. Ric has a good job with the electrical service, but we could never have afforded staterooms in first class if it wasn't for them."

"Lois, honestly," Mr. Long chided sharply. "Must every thought that goes through your head come straight out of your mouth?"

"I'm not ashamed that we aren't rich," Mrs. Long told her husband. It sounded like an oft-repeated phrase.

Rosemary attempted to smooth over the awkward situation. "As well you shouldn't be," she affirmed and then deftly changed the subject. "You have a beautiful family. Such a handsome son and two lovely daughters." She smiled in the direction of the tow-headed girls.

"That's Franny; she's the youngest. Rose is seven, and

our son, Stewie, is thirteen," Lois explained proudly.

"It's Stewart, Mum," the boy said in the same sharp tone his father had used before.

Mrs. Long waved off the comment exactly the way she had her husband's. "Yes, yes, of course, dear."

Rosemary extended a hand to the eldest daughter. "We have something in common. You're Rose, and I'm Rosemary."

The girl looked back at her with curiosity and suspicion. She was no pushover, but careful and precocious. Still, she must have seen something she liked because she smiled and shook Rosemary's hand.

"Would you like to see my drawing?" Rose asked with a slight lisp, then smiled sweetly, revealing a gap where she had recently lost one of her baby teeth. She pulled a folded-up sheet of paper from her pocket and opened it carefully.

Expecting to see a child's scribble or perhaps a clumsily drawn woodland animal, Rosemary was surprised by a beautiful seascape sketched in a style reminiscent of Vincent van Gogh's Starry Night. It was Southampton docks seen through a ship's porthole, with the initials RL carved into the frame. The little girl was already signing her work!

"Wow," Rosemary said, astounded. "You're amazing—a natural talent."

"Isn't she?" Mrs. Long said proudly. "I don't know

where she gets it from. Neither her father nor I have any artistic skill to speak of, do we, dear?" Mr. Long seemed to notice his wife was speaking to him rather than having paid any attention to what she'd actually said and merely nodded in agreement.

"I'm an artist, too," Rosemary told the girl, for once amused rather than suspicious of the concept of coincidence.

Before long the family gathered themselves and excused themselves in search of entertainment on one of the upper decks. Young Stewart went reluctantly, loath to end his conversation with Frederick, which, Rosemary had gathered from snippets, had regarded the finer points of American baseball, a subject she hadn't known her brother to have taken any interest in before.

"Boys his age always take to Freddie," Desmond joked when Rosemary pointed out the fact, "because they're both of the same maturity level."

"Not so, Desi-boy," Frederick replied easily, using a nickname from their childhood that he knew Desmond loathed. "Children simply recognize a good person instinctively. Like dogs or horses."

Rosemary admired her brother's ability to turn an insult into a positive, even when he was forced to grasp at straws.

Desmond turned his attention to Vera. "Children recognize kindred spirits, and nobody's a bigger child than Freddie. Do you think that will make it easier or harder when you have some of your own?"

Vera's eyebrows shot to her forehead, and she choked on her last bite of egg.

"Are you quite all right, Vera?" Rosemary offered her friend a whack between the shoulder blades to help ease the choking, a small smile playing around her lips.

Still sharp, even in her diminished state, Vera cleared her throat and shot a glare in Rosemary's direction. "Whatever are you wearing?" she fired back, changing the subject entirely. "What happened to all of your lovely dresses?"

"Your guess is as good as mine," Rosemary explained, taking pity and dropping the subject of children in favor of Vera's favorite topic: fashion. "Neither of you has seen my garment bag, I suppose?"

Frederick took a deep breath and let it out on a sigh. "If I have to hear one more word about garment bags, haute couture, or the proper length of a summer skirt, I will take a flying leap off the Boat Deck."

"Your suicide might bring down the mood of Vera's shuffleboard match," Desmond quipped, then laughed along with Frederick at his own joke.

Ignoring the men, Vera asked Rosemary, "Has some of your luggage gone missing? Come to think of it, I haven't seen my hat boxes anywhere."

"They're behind the pile of trunks, dear," Frederick

interjected. "It's all there, so could you kindly cease with the obsession?"

Continuing to ignore her husband, Vera turned to Desmond, "And your things?"

"I've only three cases and a trunk, Vera; there wasn't much to lose," Desmond replied with a roll of his eyes. "Perhaps the steward became overwhelmed by the sheer volume of baggage and erroneously placed some of Rose's items with the rest of your trunks in the cargo hold. Perhaps he considered it a hazard to fill your suite to the ceiling with cases."

"Or perhaps Mother was right, and we've been the victims of a grand scheme to divest wealthy travelers of their fripperies," Frederick suggested jovially, earning himself a glare. "You must admit, darling, you would serve as rather a prime target."

CHAPTER NINE

Vera insisted on getting the lie of the land, which to her mind meant securing deck chairs on the promenade and watching the entrance vestibule in anticipation of Mirella Verratti's arrival.

"Do you think we're getting too old to guzzle giggle water from dusk to dawn?" Vera pressed the heel of her hand to her temple. When that didn't settle the ache, she undid the drawstring bag she'd hung over the back of the chair and pulled out a pair of dark glasses.

After a moment, Vera tipped up the glasses and fixed her gaze on Rosemary's face. "Why don't you look as miserable as I feel?"

"I didn't stay up until dawn, or did you forget?" she replied, quite enjoying a rare upper hand.

Rosemary knew Vera would find the fortitude for shuffleboard if it meant hobnobbing with celebrities but suspected that the interlude of fresh air and tea was also necessary to clear her friend's pounding head.

Given Molly the stewardess' instruction to do just that—spend some time above decks—if she felt woozy from the motion, Rosemary wasn't one to complain. Even Frederick and Desmond had settled in for an afternoon of lounging, content not to exert themselves overmuch.

Before too long, their group was joined by Trix McCoy, who still seemed somewhat leery of Vera after her sharp comment at the dinner table, but also content to socialize mainly with those passengers from her own compartment. Probably, those she deemed to be of a similar station, Rosemary surmised.

Trix carried a notebook and pencil with her. Every so often, she made a point of pulling out a sharpener in the shape of a ship's helm—probably purchased in one of the onboard shops—and twisting the pencil exactly seven times. Rosemary knew because she counted. In between bouts of pencil twisting, Trix jotted copious notes that looked like chicken scratch from Rosemary's side-eye view.

Nobody spoke for several minutes, Miss McCoy busy scribbling, Vera and Desmond nursing headaches, and Frederick enjoying a rare moment of silence as he breathed in the salty sea air and lay back against the lounge chair, quite at ease. Rosemary brightened when she saw Mr. Tait sauntering down the promenade, a young lady at his side.

"Good morning, Mr. Tait," she called, noting he wore the same bleary-eyed expression as the rest of those suffering from an evening of excess.

"I trust you're feeling better this morning—" he checked his wristwatch, noting it was near-on noon "— or what accounts for morning amongst the leisure class."

Rosemary nodded. "Much better, yes. Thank you for your kindness last night, by the way."

"I know exactly how you can repay me," Mr. Tait said and indicated his companion. "This is Hattie Humphries, from the berth next to mine. She's traveling alone, and while I'm certain she has no objection to my titillating company, I also suspect she'd prefer to converse with like-minded ladies rather than an increasingly decrepit old man. Would you mind entertaining her for the afternoon?"

Hattie Humphries certainly appeared more than capable of entertaining herself but raised an eyebrow hopefully. "Of course, it's nice to meet you, Hattie," Rosemary said, taking pity on the girl and motioning for her to claim an empty lounge chair.

"Splendid," said Mr. Tait. "Now, I'm absolutely famished, so I think I'll just find myself something to eat. Perhaps they'll still be serving those delightful fried potatoes." With that, he was off, leaving Hattie in the awkward position of making small talk with a group of strangers.

Vera was, of course, quite welcoming and, combined with Rosemary's genial nature, tended to put people at ease quickly. And yet, it was the author with whom Hattie appeared taken.

"You're *the* Trix McCoy?" she asked, her eyes wide and sparkling. "The author of *Mrs. Willoughby and the Poisoned Pen*?" Hattie gushed. "I enjoyed your book, Miss McCoy—truly, it was nothing short of genius." Vera returned to her fashion magazine with a shrug.

"Why thank you ever so much," the author replied, clearly basking in the praise. Who could blame the lady for feeling flattered? "Would you like me to autograph your copy?" she asked, bringing a smile and then an immediate frown to Hattie's face.

"Unfortunately, I haven't brought it with me," she lamented.

Miss McCoy appeared somewhat miffed at the admission but offered generously, "I'll just get my secretary to find you a new one. Here he comes now."

Dolph had indeed appeared, ambling from the same direction Mr. Tait had come, and while he looked to be in better shape than most of the passengers who'd overindulged, he still carried shadows below his eyes, giving the faint impression of ill health.

"Dolph, be a dear and fetch a copy of my novel for Miss Humphries," Trix commanded, seemingly oblivious to the notion that it might further put him out to trek back to her stateroom.

However, instead of retracing his steps, Dolph sat down in the empty chair next to his employer and pulled a copy of her book from his shoulder bag. "No need to fetch anything as I've come prepared."

Rosemary managed to hold back a snort, but just barely.

"I've also swapped rooms already; all of your things are just as you like them." Dolph's voice trailed off as he searched the shoulder bag more urgently. "I must have left my notebook back in the suite. I suppose I'll have to go back, after all, to fetch it."

Miss McCoy waved a hand to stop him from getting to his feet. "You're always misplacing things."

Mr. Sutton acknowledged the truth of her statement with a sheepish expression. "I may have to go down to the cargo hold to retrieve the spare glass steam tube for my inhaler."

Not seeming terribly concerned for his health, his employer merely shrugged. "I'm certain both items will turn up. Things usually do. Thank you for swapping our rooms. Perhaps I'll sleep tonight," she said gratefully and then explained to them all, even though nobody had asked, that "some sort of racket from the common area" had kept her up all night.

Not having heard a peep even though her room also butted up against the common area, Rosemary was stumped and decided perhaps the author was just an incredibly light sleeper. She seemed to possess a striking number of peculiarities, but Rosemary supposed that was just the way it was with writers—they weren't often labeled eccentric for no reason.

Hattie, understandably, had perked up noticeably at Dolph's arrival. "It seems we're neighbors," she said, and had she been a more brazen girl, Rosemary suspected she would have batted her eyelashes.

When he didn't take the bait, greeting her politely but then turning to speak with Rosemary, Miss Humphries appeared somewhat put out. Her lip jutted slightly, and a crease appeared between her brow—but she maintained a pasted smile and instead turned back to the author.

"Miss McCoy, are you working on your next book?" Hattie asked, evidently unable to curb her curiosity.

Miss McCoy smiled, set her notebook on the tray to her left, and picked up the copy of the *Poisoned Pen* to autograph for Hattie. "Yes, as a matter of fact. The next one is to be set on an ocean liner, actually, so as you can imagine, this voyage is rife with material for my plot."

Rosemary found it unlikely Hattie had expected the floodgates to open, but the author seemed content to wax on about her work.

"It's not only writing, you know," she said, waving around the pen. "People always think a story comes to a writer fully formed, but that's rarely the case. Most often, it's a snippet, just the fragment of an idea, and then you must tend it—like a garden. You must water it, nurture it, speak to it, and let it speak to you. Let your characters speak to you. Just one good idea isn't enough. It isn't a plot!" Miss McCoy let out a rehearsed-sounding giggle. "And then again, plot isn't to be confused with story, is it?"

Hattie listened with rapt attention, but Rosemary lost interest and returned her attention to Dolph. An author's life didn't sound terribly titillating, after all, if it included haranguing strangers into listening about the creative process.

Indeed, Trix McCoy sounded like Vera when someone asked about her work as an actress. *You have to be your character*, Rosemary could almost hear her friend say. Then she realized that they both likely came across the same way she did when she started talking about color choice and brush technique!

She had to admit that her art hadn't been a priority as of late. If she had to speak about anything with authority, it would be means, motive, and opportunity for murder—a topic that would likely be quite welcome in the present company but one which Rosemary loathed to bring up.

Enamored, Hattie pressed Trix further. "So what's the plot—or the story?" she asked, clearly still uncertain as to the difference between the two. "Who are you going

73

to kill off?"

"Oh, I can't tell you that, now can I?" Trix said with a grin in Dolph's direction. "You'll have to buy the book!"

The secretary watched Hattie's pretty face fall and took pity, revealing he wasn't perhaps as impervious to her looks as he'd appeared. "Certainly, Trix, you can give her a little something to chew on," Dolph cajoled.

It didn't take much to convince the author. "Oh, all right," she said. "I suppose it won't hurt to tell you a little about the subplot." Miss McCoy lowered her voice, forcing anyone who cared enough to lean in closer to hear what she had to say. "My sleuth gets caught up in the middle of an American rum-smuggling operation! She singlehandedly foils the dastardly plan, of course, but at what cost?" Now Miss McCoy sounded like she was reading the description from the back of the novel.

Hattie gasped, her dark eyes wide, and then a slow smile spread across her face. "How smashing! How very American!"

"Oh no, Miss McCoy," Frederick interjected from out of nowhere. Even Rosemary was surprised he'd been paying attention. With his hat pulled down over his eyes, she'd assumed he was napping. "Don't have her foil the rum-smuggling plot. Those poor Americans have suffered enough! Your Miss What's-her-name should let them get clear away."

Hattie stared at Frederick. "With murder?" she asked, incredulous.

"Of course not," Frederick replied. "Just with the running of the rum. I would never advocate murder," he insisted.

At that, the mystery author tutted. "Everyone is capable of murder, Mr. Woolridge, if the circumstances are just so."

Frederick shook his head, serious now. "I didn't say I wasn't capable; I said I wouldn't advocate it. Trust me, murder is far more grisly in real life than it is printed on the pages of a book."

Again, Hattie's mouth dropped open, Rosemary's snapped tightly shut, and then she shot her brother a quelling look.

The moment she'd heard Trix McCoy was a murder mystery author, Rosemary had decided to keep her involvement in real-life investigations to herself. She intended to enjoy this trip, and no response, be it interest or some sort of challenge, sounded as though it would aid in achieving that goal. What Rosemary knew was there would be a reaction, which would require an explanation, which was the last thing she wanted to give.

Oblivious, Frederick pressed on. "Rosie here is practically engaged to one of the top detectives in all of London. We've been privy to plenty of investigations and—"

"Frederick, you're exaggerating again," Rosemary said pointedly. He received an elbow in the ribs from his wife when Vera caught on to Rosemary's reluctance. Frederick shut his mouth, finally realizing his gaffe, and Miss McCoy didn't press, but Rosemary noticed Hattie glancing at her inquisitively for the rest of the afternoon.

Blessedly, though, the conversation drifted. In fact, it came to a halt for a brief while, with everyone engrossed in their individual tasks or focused on the activities happening nearby. Rosemary took the opportunity to observe the deck, taking a moment to absorb the fine detail.

It seemed as though a significant portion of the first-class passengers had flocked to the promenade to enjoy the sunshine. Even though there was still a breeze, young ladies sunned themselves in rows of lounge chairs, preening for the gentleman. Rosemary felt a sense of familiarity with the situation and puzzled over the notion for a moment before recalling a childhood trip to London Zoo, where she'd watched a group of ostriches behave in precisely the same fashion.

Desmond peered at the line of prettily painted ladies with some interest. "Be careful," the vigilant Hattie warned. "Those women might be lined up like vultures on a branch, but they aren't vultures; they're sharks, and they only eat fresh meat."

Desmond returned the statement with a quizzical

expression.

"I recognize the type," Hattie explained.

Mr. Sutton seemed to agree. "She's right, you know," he said. "Have you any idea how many eligible bachelors can be found puffing Cubans in the first-class smoking room? This ship is a floating nightclub that never closes. I've seen more than one unsuspecting businessman meet a lovely lady at the Observation Lounge bar on the first night aboard ship, get entirely swept away in the romance, and insist on being married by the captain before arriving at port! I've also seen the same gentleman traveling second-class six months later after his new wife's fleeced him for all he's worth!"

It was a thought that stuck with Rosemary for the rest of the afternoon, even after Vera dragged Frederick off for a peek at the Verratti couple, and Miss McCoy, Mr. Sutton, and their new shadow, Hattie, had packed up and gone in search of warmer climes.

"She's the one I have to watch out for," Desmond said when Hattie was out of earshot.

With a glance at the young lady's retreating back, Rosemary tilted her head to one side. "She does have a damsel-in-distress air about her, which always has been your type."

"It's every man's type, Rosie," Desmond replied. "We just can't resist. Say, perhaps I ought to chuck the chivalrous persona altogether," he mused, "since all it seems to cause is grief. Life would be much easier if one didn't have to worry about being gentlemanly or tactful or polite. I envy folks who can simply say 'sod off' without a care or a second thought."

Reminded of the similar statement she'd made regarding Vera's personality, Rosemary nodded in agreement even though she knew Desmond no more capable of it than she, and posed the question, "Why not just give one of these girls a chance? Surely you don't find every female here completely abhorrent?"

When Desmond appeared doubtful, she pressed, "Or is there someone else, in the States, on whom you've set your sights?" He'd been uncharacteristically mum on the subject, and Rosemary was dying to know what had transpired during his last trip to America.

He pierced her with an odd expression she chose to interpret as benign and nodded. "Yes, Rosemary, I have another in my sights, as you say," he said lightly and shifted his gaze forward. "But I suppose you're right; there's no harm in giving these girls a chance to woo me." Desmond lifted himself out of his chair and sauntered over to a trio of coquettish smiles, tossing a wink back in Rosemary's direction.

Realizing she might have made a fatal error in judgment by getting involved in the first place, she decided to keep all future notions regarding Desmond's love life to herself. His interest in her she viewed, at this point, as merely a passing fancy despite his comment. After all, Desmond was clearly resilient and furthermore tended to bore easily. Someone else would catch his eye before long, just as someone always did.

For a few pleasant moments, Rosemary was left alone with her thoughts, and she took the time to look around and appreciate the experience of sailing—if zipping through the ocean at twenty-five knots could be considered sailing. Despite it being technically summertime, the route between Southampton and New York skewed north into colder waters, and the breeze carried the promise of a chill to come. She drew in a breath of fresh sea air and vowed to enjoy the warmer weather for as long as it lasted.

When Vera and Frederick returned, she wore a disappointed expression, and he had his arm around her comfortingly. "It's all right, darling. You'll get another chance."

"No, I won't," Vera insisted petulantly. Rosemary applauded her brother for his newfound patience and wondered what sort of error in judgment he'd made that required buttering up his wife. "Tomorrow, it will be too cold for shuffleboard, and I'll have lost my chance to befriend Mirella Verratti!"

"How will the world keep turning," Desmond said dispassionately, having returned to the group during the middle of Vera's lament, "if you're unable to befriend

Mirella Verratti? You know there are starving children in Africa, don't you, Vera?"

Vera tilted her nose in the air and retorted, "There are starving children in England, as well; war, pestilence, murder, and all manner of duplicity besides. Somehow, we all seem to find ways to enjoy ourselves despite the horrors. Even you, Desmond dear, or perhaps especially you," she said pointedly.

Desmond laughed heartily and jabbed the air near Vera with his elbow in a gesture of camaraderie, but she duly ignored him, which only served to amuse him further.

"The worst part is, I've overheard three people say they'd bet money she and Mr. Verratti are on the outs and that's why they've been holed up in their suite all day. According to the stewardess, they had quite a row."

Rosemary tilted her head to one side curiously. "Aren't they staying in the Millionaires' Suites?" she asked, assuming correctly her friend knew the answer to the question.

"Yes, that's right. One of the nicest berths, just on the other side of the shops, with a private promenade," Vera confirmed. "What difference does that make?"

"Nothing, I suppose. Only, I expected the best rooms would have the best service and therefore the best stewardess—not one who would be willing to break a passenger's confidence." Rosemary recounted her experiences with Molly. "I can't imagine that behavior would be tolerated by the steward supervisor. Perhaps it was merely a rumor amongst the other passengers. There's probably little truth to it," she said in an attempt at reassurance.

Vera brightened infinitesimally at the suggestion. "Perhaps you're right. And you know what else? She'll be stuck inside with the rest of us when it's too cold for the upper decks. I'll find a way to speak to her then."

And so all wasn't lost for Vera. At least, not until Desmond chimed, "I, for one, believe it. They don't make any sense as a couple. Hey Freddie, you think there's someone on board offering stakes on a breakup?"

"Not sure," Frederick replied, "but I suspect the odds will be definitively in our favor!"

Chapter Ten

Dinner on the second night aboard the ship was just as sumptuous as it had been the first, causing Vera to declare forlornly, "If I'm not careful, by the time we arrive in America, none of my clothes will fit! Starting tomorrow, I'm taking the stairs between decks."

"I'll admit, there's merit to your concern," Rosemary replied, "but I don't regret one morsel of my roast duckling and gooseberry tart!"

Some short time later, she and her friends had settled into a corner of B Deck's Winter Garden Lounge, along with several of the other passengers from their section. Rosemary couldn't recall which of her neighbors had mentioned congregating there, but it seemed they'd all taken the suggestion to heart.

The lounge, decorated in a jungle theme with potted palms, silk brocade wallpaper featuring the types of animals one might find on safari—tigers, giraffes, zebras—and bamboo-trimmed furniture was the epitome of casual elegance.

Beneath a swath of fronds, at a cluster of cushioned armchairs positioned around a low coffee table, lounged Miss McCoy, Hattie, and the Longs. Mr. Tait sat in a chair in the corner, opposite Rosemary and perpendicular to the rest of the group. He presumed to be reading but every so often would look up and assess the rest of the group. Rosemary doubted he'd secured that seat by accident; it let him observe without obligation to participate.

Miss McCoy wore a pair of magnifying glasses and worked an embroidery needle furiously while somehow simultaneously keeping tabs on the room. Her gaze flicked quickly around, landing only occasionally on the piece in her hands and causing Rosemary to wonder if she wasn't more intent on cataloging the movements of all the other passengers than she was on completing her needlework.

The two of them, Rosemary thought—Mr. Tait and Miss McCoy—would make the perfect match! Both of a similar age and disposition, perhaps the notion wasn't entirely out of the question. Then, she remembered how quickly Mr. Tait had left the dinner table the evening before and his general reluctance to socialize and decided perhaps not. A pity, in her opinion.

At a nearby corner table raged a spirited game of bridge. The female half of the couple Rosemary had noticed the previous evening but had not yet officially met—the Parsons if she remembered correctly—presided over the game.

Miss McCoy's eyes narrowed slightly when they caught Mrs. Long gazing rather longingly at the match over the top of her copy of *Mrs. Willoughby and the Poisoned Pen*, and Rosemary had to stifle a laugh. Perhaps it was a writer's trait to observe, or perhaps her occupation was merely an excuse for inherent nosiness.

Rosemary's gaze flicked to Mr. Tait, his amused expression mirroring her own, and she realized he'd also caught on to Miss McCoy's irritation. He winked at Rosemary before returning to his own book, a thick volume of indeterminate genre she highly doubted featured an intrepid lady sleuth!

Mr. Long, on the other hand, gazed rather longingly at the cigar clutched by Mr. Parsons, his wife forgotten. Mr. Parsons caught the eye of Mr. Long, reached into his jacket pocket, and pulled out a duplicate cigar, keeping his finger over the band. "If you can name the brand, it's yours," he said loudly, waving it in the general direction of Mr. Long's face and receiving an arched eyebrow in response.

"That's a Lords of England," Mr. Long replied, his eyes never leaving the other man's. "It will have the flavor of both oak and nuts with a fair amount of spice."

A long moment of tension followed, where even

Rosemary realized she'd been holding her breath until Mr. Parsons let out a boisterous laugh and clapped Mr. Long on the back as he proffered the prize.

Then, he turned to Frederick and Desmond. The pair stared, unashamedly, at the cigars like two trained hounds catching the scent of a wild hare. "You gentlemen interested in another round of wagers?" Mr. Parsons asked with a suggestive wiggle of his brows. "I promised my wife I'd be her partner this evening, but the smoking room up on the Promenade Deck is where you want to be."

Vera pierced her husband with a concerned look. "Freddie, darling, are you quite sure that's wise?" she cajoled.

"I'm on holiday, *Vera darling*, and I do plan to enjoy myself to the same extent I expect you to enjoy my account at the shops. Now, stop fussing and kiss me before I stink like a cigar."

Rosemary noticed the vein in her friend's temple begin to throb, but Vera smoothed her face into a smile and said, "Very well."

"To the smoking room, then," Frederick said as though he were headed out to storm a castle, and then he and Desmond made a hasty exit behind Mr. Long, expecting quite naturally that the ladies would manage just fine on their own.

As soon as the men were gone, Mrs. Parsons

approached Mrs. Long and asked, "Would you like to join the game?"

It was all the prompting Mrs. Long required, and she excused herself to the bridge table, the *Poisoned Pen* abandoned on her seat. Miss McCoy avoided gazing directly at the novel, pretending not to notice or care, but she wasn't fooling Rosemary. Unless she was quite mistaken, the author had taken some offense.

"I have always wondered," Hattie leaned toward Miss McCoy as if expecting to be the recipient of confidential information, "where authors get their ideas. How do you decide who to kill, and how do you come up with such inventive methods of murder?"

With the longsuffering look of someone who has been asked the same questions many times over, Miss McCoy launched into what felt to Rosemary like an explanation by rote. One designed to satisfy curiosity without giving away her secrets.

Hattie kept the author talking until Dolph appeared and took a seat to Miss McCoy's right. "Good evening, Rosemary," he said shyly, "Miss Humphries, Trix. You all look lovely this evening."

"How lovely it must be for you to be on such familiar terms with your employer," Hattie declared unexpectedly. Had the comment come from anyone else, it might have sounded pointed, but the girl's wide eyes and innocent expression left little doubt that she simply lacked any verbal acuity. An ingénue, Rosemary's mother would have called Hattie, but with a bite to her tone.

Miss McCoy stared daggers at her, but Hattie hardly noticed, instead turning her attention to Mr. Sutton and proving she hadn't meant any harm. "It must be an extraordinary honor to work with someone so talented." The author appeared somewhat mollified.

"I did quite think it would be a nice, quiet job, and then, well, the book became a bestseller, and now it's a constant whirlwind," Mr. Sutton explained. "Not that I'm complaining, of course," he was quick to add.

Hattie let out a laugh that roused even Mr. Tait, who glanced up and harrumphed with a disapproving expression.

The author smiled, pleased, and said sincerely, "I couldn't have done it without your help."

"Perhaps," Dolph accepted the praise with modesty, "but you're the one who put in the hard work. You took a snippet of an idea and turned it into a complex, multifaceted mystery. If you don't believe me, just ask any of your countless fans. All I did was decipher your admittedly terrible penmanship."

The conversation continued in that vein for a while until Dolph yawned for the second time and excused himself to his stateroom.

Vera had long since lost interest, as she tended to do

when she wasn't the center of attention. Mrs. Long had left the bridge table, leaving an opening Vera was quick to snap up. "I think I'll join in the game if you don't mind," she said to Rosemary, excusing herself to the table with a glint in her eye. "What's sauce for the goose is sauce for the gander, isn't that what they say?"

"Have fun," Rosemary called out. Mr. Tait watched the exchange over the top of his book and then nodded in Vera's direction. "Will her husband regret leaving her to her own devices?" he asked Rosemary, raising his voice enough to be heard from his seat on the other side of the armchairs.

Rosemary shook her head. "Not in the way you'd think. She won't lose to make him angry; she'll win, significantly more than he will and then demand to be worshiped for her cunning. That's Vera's modus operandi."

Hattie continued firing questions at Miss McCoy, listening to her answers with rapt attention. The author appeared to have forgotten her earlier annoyance with the young lady and basked in the praise.

"Well, Rosie, I think I may have lost my touch when it comes to bridge," Vera said upon her return. "I've lost more than that, actually. These women take their betting quite seriously. Freddie will be furious, but he'll lose too and won't have a leg to stand on, so I suppose I win either way." She shrugged and reached for Rosemary's hand. "I'm exhausted. Have you nearly finished?"

Rosemary welcomed the opportunity to leave the conversation, feeling no remorse for leaving Hattie with Miss McCoy. She had, after all, been the one to instigate the discussion regarding the author's success, and therefore she ought to be the one forced to listen to the tale in its entirety.

"I'm ready. Let's go." She and Vera locked arms, and Rosemary bent her head towards her dearest friend and asked, "Did you really overdo it, or were you showing mercy to me and staged a daring rescue?"

Vera grinned and replied cheekily, "A little bit of both! Let's go and find a cigarette stand and a couple of G&Ts." She pulled Rosemary towards the lift, which was just beginning to close. The heels Vera so adored proved too high to move very quickly, and they arrived just in time to see the lift take off carrying none other than the coveted Verrattis.

Mr. Verratti held his wife in his arms as though she were a delicate flower and gazed deep into her eyes. Instead of capturing her lips in a kiss, he pulled her into the crook of his arm and held her there, tenderly, as they were whisked upwards. As lovely a moment as it might have been, Rosemary knew her friend would have gladly interrupted it if it meant sharing a lift with the object of her obsession.

"Perhaps we ought to have worn flat shoes" Rosemary

said and received a sharp elbow to the ribs she didn't have time to avoid.

"What would be the fun in that?" Vera wanted to know.

"Oh, I don't know, maybe the ability to tell if we still have toes by the end of an evening."

"You really are an old married woman at heart, aren't you, Rosie?" One or two drinks past the point where her brain and her mouth worked at the same speed, Vera didn't intend her words to wound, but that didn't stop the quick stab to Rosemary's heart.

"Maybe so."

By now, the lift had returned, and once inside, Rosemary decided she'd had enough revelry for one night. Her shoes did, in fact, pinch her feet, and the trim of her frock had begun to rub her skin tender. "Would you be horribly upset if I passed up that G&T?"

"Are you quite well?" Vera's immediate concern went a long way toward easing the ache she'd caused.

"I am," she said with a warm hug for her friend. "Just a little tired, that's all."

And so, with Vera's blessing, Rosemary returned to her stateroom where she kicked off the offending shoes, slumped into the nearest chair, and wriggled her toes to bring back some of the feeling into them.

Enjoying the silence, Rosemary almost fell asleep in the chair and was just getting ready for bed when the lights flickered and nearly went out.

"I shall take that as a sign," Rosemary said to no one and slid between the sheets.

CHAPTER ELEVEN

Rosemary found her second night aboard the ship far more pleasant than the first. Her stomach settled into the rhythm of the waves, and the bouts of nausea decreased to only the occasional pang. Still, she woke early, just as she tended to do on land, never having needed much sleep to feel rested—a fact that galled Vera, who coveted her beauty sleep.

Fortunately, the ship was akin to a floating city, operating at all hours of the day and night to accommodate its passengers' myriad needs and desires. Breakfast wouldn't be served in the Grand Saloon quite yet, but the Winter Garden Lounge on the other side of the first-class entrance would already have tea and toast on offer for the early risers.

After performing another futile search for the bag of sport dresses, Rosemary concluded they must have indeed been misplaced and checked the ship directory. She took note of where the Enquiry Office was located, two floors up on the Boat Deck, and vowed to call in later and report her missing suitcase.

She had nearly finished pinning her hair into a stylish yet simple twist when a noise from one of the other compartments pierced the early-morning silence. It sounded like a woman's garbled scream and set the hairs on the back of Rosemary's neck to attention.

No concerned gasps or muffled footsteps followed, and she came quite close to simply brushing off the sense of foreboding that had accompanied the sound but ultimately decided she had better investigate.

Rosemary opened the stateroom door and peered into the hallway, which was still deserted and dimly lit this early in the morning, straining her ears for any suspicious noises. Based on the direction of the sound, she concluded it had come not from Desmond's cabin, positioned next to hers, but from across the hall where Miss McCoy and her secretary were stationed in the staterooms originally assigned to herself and Anna.

One of the doors had been left open a crack, and it took Rosemary a moment to remember whose room it was. Miss McCoy had been across from her the first night, but she had swapped with Dolph the day before. The author's door was the one ajar, she realized, and so Rosemary tapped lightly and then poked her head inside.

"Miss McCoy," she called, loudly enough that someone on the other side ought to hear her but not so loud as to wake the whole compartment.

When she heard no reply, Rosemary considered retreating, but her heartbeat quickened as she replayed the sound of the cry in her head. Why was the door ajar? Could Miss McCoy have injured herself somehow? Was she lying inside, unconscious or in distress? Deciding safety was more important than propriety, Rosemary entered the stateroom only to discover, anticlimactically, that it was empty.

Either it hadn't been Miss McCoy she'd heard after all, or perhaps the author had joined Mr. Sutton in his room. If that were the case, it would be impertinent to interrupt. She left the door open a crack, just as she'd found it, and nearly walked away, putting the whole thing out of her mind, but something about that noise had rattled her nerves. Rosemary found she had no choice but to follow her curiosity through to its conclusion.

It was an inclination that had betrayed her on numerous occasions, yet one which she seemed quite unable to ignore.

"Mr. Sutton, Miss McCoy," she called, knocking lightly. "It's Rosemary Lillywhite from across the hall. Are you both quite all right?"

The sound of someone clearing her throat echoed from inside the stateroom, and then Rosemary heard Miss McCoy say, "Help, please," noting almost in passing that she sounded resigned rather than injured or hysterical.

"What's the matter?" Rosemary asked as she came round the corner, stopping short when she saw the answer to her question without the author needing to say another word.

Dolph Sutton, who Rosemary had quite liked, lay sprawled on the floor, his complexion even paler than it had been in life. He appeared to have fallen out of his desk chair, and blessedly, his eyes were closed, creating a sense he might just have been deeply sleeping and not dead as a doornail.

Except Rosemary knew, deep down in the pit of her stomach, that was exactly what he was. Poor Dolph, she thought to herself—the last fleeting thought before she shoved her emotions to the back of her mind and did what had to be done.

"I'm terribly sorry, Miss McCoy, truly," Rosemary said, rousing the author, who finally tore her eyes away from the dead man's face.

"He's just—he just needs his inhaler." She gestured towards the apparatus sitting on top of the desk. All gleaming brass and glass, the cylindrical burner and breathing tube looked like a mad chemist's idea of a teapot. "He's just having a spell."

Clearly, Miss McCoy wasn't as accustomed to finding dead bodies as Rosemary was and had yet to grasp the gravity of the circumstances. Her composure never wavering, Rosemary stepped over Dolph's legs, as respectfully as she could, and hauled Miss McCoy into a standing position—not an easy feat given the woman's stature and build, but Rosemary could feel adrenaline coursing through her veins.

"Come with me, please, Miss McCoy," she said, but the other woman still couldn't work out how to move her feet. "Trix!" Rosemary snapped, trying a different tactic. "There's nothing you can do for him now except notify the authorities. We really must go."

Just as Rosemary decided the last resort was to give her a good slap across the face, Miss McCoy seemed to come out of her stupor. She nodded a couple of times and followed Rosemary out of the stateroom. It felt surreal to discover the hallway remained empty, the rooms still quiet after what she'd just witnessed. Nothing had changed on the other side of the door.

Rosemary felt a sense of relief that proved short-lived when the young Long girl, Rose, came wandering around the corner from the common room, a well-loved teddy bear clutched in one hand. "What are you doing here, sweetie?" Rosemary asked, hoping Rose didn't notice Trix McCoy's ashen face.

"Just e'sploring," she replied, the gap from her missing tooth slurring her speech in a most adorable fashion. Under normal circumstances, Rosemary wouldn't have been able to keep the smile from her face, but just then, it was forced.

"You know what I saw, just down that way?" Rosemary said, leaning close, "A potted palm tree with the most interesting shapes to the leaves. Maybe you could draw it for me?" She ducked into her stateroom, pulled a sketchbook and charcoal pencil from the top of the desk, and returned in a flash to hand them over to Rose. The little girl stared greedily at the thick ream of paper. "Run along now," Rosemary urged, and she didn't have to say it twice.

Blessedly, one of the stewards—the one who had shown them to their compartments upon boarding the ship in Southampton—came round the corner, whistling a tune that cut off abruptly when he noted the expressions on the two ladies' faces.

"Stratford, was it?" Rosemary asked, and he nodded.

"How can I help you?"

"There's been an accident in Mr. Sutton's room." Rosemary lowered her voice. "He seems to have had an asthma attack, and died, sometime last night, by my best guess."

Stratford's forehead creased deeply, and his eyes flicked between Rosemary and Miss McCoy. To her credit, the tip of the author's nose lifted into the air defiantly, and all trace of distress disappeared from her face, leaving it a stony mask.

When the steward realized this wasn't the ramblings of a pair of hysterical women, his Adam's apple bobbled around for a moment, and then he strode through the stateroom door as if still not entirely convinced of what he would find.

It only took a moment for Stratford to reappear, his cheeks flaming and his brow drawn even further together. "You two ought to return to your staterooms. I'll alert the doctor." When neither Rosemary nor Miss McCoy moved an inch, he sighed, shrugged, and went off down the hall to the telephone.

"I'm very sorry for your loss," Rosemary said to Miss McCoy when he was out of earshot. "Is there anything I can do for you?"

The author stared straight ahead, only sparing Rosemary a quick glance, and shook her head. "No, thank you." Her voice didn't waver now, confirming Rosemary's estimation of Trix McCoy as a strong, resilient woman. "Together, we'd found the perfect working relationship. You have no idea how rare that is. I can't imagine who will keep me on deadline now," she said in a tone that struck Rosemary as sad, with a bitter undertone. It was her loss to bear, and therefore Rosemary chose not to judge. She knew better than anyone that when confronted with death, people ran a gamut of emotions often misunderstood by those less affected by the loss.

Far faster than Rosemary had expected, Captain Hughes arrived. A tall man with salt-and-pepper hair and stern eyes, he wore a uniform quite similar in some ways to those of the stewards with the same lapel pin, but with more stripes on the sleeves and a bit more decoration on his hat. The captain exuded competency. Exactly the thing one wanted to see in the man in charge of such a crossing.

He got right to the point. "What's happened here?"

"A man has died." Rosemary gestured towards Mr. Sutton's stateroom.

"We'll let the doctor be the judge of that, shall we?" The captain's gaze flicked past Rosemary as he strode to the door and assessed the situation.

"If you please, Doctor Eastman."

After stepping back to let the doctor have access to Mr. Sutton's prone form, the captain removed himself to the doorway where he stood, arms crossed over his chest, watching the proceedings.

Doctor Eastman wasted little time in making the pronouncement. "This man is dead."

Just in time, since the captain had turned in her direction, Rosemary schooled her expression into one that read more *I'm sorry,* than *I told you so*.

The captain merely nodded, then left the doorway to find a steward and stretcher.

"I'm very sorry for your loss." The doctor repeated

Rosemary's earlier sentiment—one Miss McCoy would become tired of hearing quite quickly. He stood and said to Miss McCoy, "Was this man your husband?"

Taking advantage of the captain's brief diversion of attention, Rosemary followed Miss McCoy into Mr. Sutton's stateroom. Not a moment too soon, as the captain returned quite quickly.

"He was not," said Miss McCoy. "We enjoyed a working relationship only."

Captain Hughes offered his sincere sympathies in a short preamble before getting straight to the point. "You were his employer?"

"Yes, he's my secretary. Was my secretary," she corrected sadly. "Randolph Sutton."

A brief examination of the scene ensued, and then Dolph's body was carefully loaded onto the stretcher. Before the doctor could cover him over with a sheet, Rosemary noticed a mark on the bottom of his foot. It looked like soot, or perhaps dirt, and for some reason, it caused her pause.

"How long has he been in your employ?" The captain resumed his fact-finding mission.

Miss McCoy thought for a moment. "Three—no, four years," she finally decided.

"And when did you last see Mr. Sutton alive?" The captain continued to work through the necessary questions.

"In the Winter Garden Lounge with the rest of the group. Dolph went to bed, and I stayed up playing bridge with some of the ladies. I assumed he'd done his evening work and gone to sleep. You see, before bed, he would take his medication and use his inhaler. Then, he'd review his notes from the day—my ramblings, things we discussed—and organize them into a notebook. Every evening, the same routine. His light was off when I passed by, so I assumed he was already sleeping. Travel did take its toll."

The doctor returned from the corridor, having followed the stretcher out, and nodded sympathetically towards Miss McCoy once more. "My inclination is to conclude Mr. Sutton suffered an asthma attack and became unable to regulate his breathing. I see he has a steam inhaler, but of course, no form of treatment is a guarantee when it comes to these types of breathing disorders."

"We'll take his identification but will leave his personal effects with you, given your relationship and the fact he's listed you as companion in the event of an emergency," Captain Hughes explained. "We'd also appreciate your discretion," he said and lowered his voice, "with regard to this matter. No need to get the other passengers in a tizzy. If you'd inform only those who will notice Mr. Sutton's absence, it would be appreciated. And of course, if there's anything we can do for you for the duration of your journey, please don't hesitate to ask."

Whether the captain didn't notice that Miss McCoy's face had turned an incensed shade of crimson or whether he simply didn't care, Rosemary couldn't say, but he beat a hasty retreat, and once again, the pair were left alone in the hallway, silence stretching between them.

"Why don't I help you back to your berth," Rosemary suggested gently, but Miss McCoy shook her head.

"Dolph would want me to tidy up," she explained. "He abhors a mess." Rosemary could tell it still hadn't sunk in that the man was gone. She had seen it before and even experienced it for herself. Denial was merely the mind's way of protecting the heart, and hers went out to Trix McCoy.

She had already gathered that the author cared for Mr. Sutton beyond the scope an employer generally would for an employee. It was precisely the same way Rosemary would have felt had it been Anna or Wadsworth, or even the relatively new cook, Gladys, who had fit seamlessly into the household right from the start. "Why don't you let me help you, then?" she suggested gently.

To her surprise, Trix capitulated, and the pair entered the stateroom together. The messy reality having been cleared, there was nothing extraordinary about the space except the extreme level of tidiness Dolph had maintained.

His bed had been meticulously made with hospital corners, turned down in a fashion not precisely matching Rosemary's, making her wonder if he had redone it himself after the maid had finished. In the wardrobe, his clothes hung, perfectly pressed and arranged by color, a muted color palette of greens and blues.

It appeared Dolph had been finishing up the last of his work and heading to bed, given what Miss McCoy had said earlier regarding his routine and confirmed by the neat stack of notebooks resting on the desk near the nebulizer. That he'd been barefoot and wearing his pajamas only served to further prove the fact. Something—some inconsistency—niggled, but she couldn't put her finger on what it might be.

Rosemary half expected Miss McCoy to sink onto the mattress or even one of the nearby chairs, but instead, she strode over to the desk and picked up a notebook from the top of the stack. She leafed through it with a sigh, swallowed hard in an attempt to stave off more tears, and then slammed it back down.

The pair made quick work of the room, neither one keen on dallying and each grateful for Dolph's particularities which, blessedly, made the task a short one. Miss McCoy carried what articles she deemed essential.

"These I'll take back to my stateroom," she declared, her voice hard, "along with his personal effects. The steward can pack his clothes and stow his luggage. I'll see it gets shipped back to his family in Devon."

It seemed all the author was capable of doing at that moment. What she needed was rest, and Rosemary said as much. "Why don't I call for the stewardess," she asked gently.

"Yes, I suppose you'd better. This is all a bit more than I expected," Miss McCoy admitted, waving a hand vaguely in the general direction of the stateroom.

Rosemary wedged open Dolph's stateroom door and deposited the author in her own accommodations along with the key and Dolph's personal belongings. She then called for Molly before returning to his room to finish tidying up.

"Are you able to keep an eye over her? I don't think she ought to be left alone."

Molly nodded and said, "Yes, Mrs. Lillywhite; I'll ask one of the other stewardesses to look after Mrs. Parsons in my stead." She didn't appear disappointed at the necessity.

Rosemary thanked the girl and returned to Dolph's room. She smoothed the bedspread, ensured all the packed cases were latched and locked, and pushed the desk chair back into place. In the process, one of the legs caught on the edge of the carpet, which had been mussed somehow, possibly during the removal of the body. Rosemary tried to lift the chair leg and reposition it, but to no avail, so she gathered her skirt and knelt down to inspect the rug.

Toward the back, her questing fingers met dampness. How very strange. Rosemary considered how one might manage to spill water in such an inaccessible spot.

As she felt around to gauge the extent of the dampness, Rosemary felt something odd beneath the carpet and traced its shape with her fingers. Frowning, she sat back on her heels for a moment to think, then leaned forward again and pressed in the middle of the oblong shape she could, now that she knew it was there, see as a slightly raised area beneath the rug. Whatever was under there gave way in the center with a muffled whumping sound.

Testing, she pressed again to get a better feel for what her mind had already labeled as evidence. Toward one end, she encountered something sharp enough to leave a shallow scratch that oozed a tiny drop of blood. Without thinking, Rosemary sucked at the sore spot and tasted salt.

Even odder.

Assuming she'd run across an errant needle from a former passenger's sewing kit, Rosemary ran ginger fingers over the spot a second time and was startled to discover not a needle but the frayed end of an electrical wire poking through the carpet's pile.

Brow wrinkled, Rosemary stood, stepped back to

observe the desk from a distance, and settled her focus on the only thing on the desk that ran on electricity: the lamp. Dread settled over her heart like a cloud settles over a valley.

Careful not to touch anything, Rosemary inspected the lamp, and specifically the wires leading from it. It wasn't easy to get into a position where she could see clearly, but her hand went to her throat when she did. Someone had cut away the cloth coating and separated the wires. Only one ran from plug to lamp. The other disappeared under the carpet, which explained why Dolph's room had been dark when Miss McCoy went to bed the previous evening.

Thinking quickly, she unplugged the lamp. Better safe than sorry when sorry was another word for dead. Hands shaking, Rosemary set the plug aside and took hold of the second set of wires. To her surprise, when she gave them a good yank, a flattened tea tray popped out from under the rug, the severed lamp wires wrapped around one side handle.

It didn't take so much as a rudimentary knowledge of electricity to see someone had taken the tray from beneath the silver tea service, and tampered with the lamp. While she wasn't sure of the exact mechanics, Rosemary knew a murder weapon when she saw one.

Hindsight being what it was, Rosemary realized the reason for her earlier niggling concern. Why would

Dolph have turned off the desk lamp, plunging himself into total darkness, if he was in the middle of using his inhaler? He wouldn't have, and he also hadn't stepped in soot or dirt. The mark on his foot had been an electrocution burn.

Dolph's death wasn't an accident. It was murder, and without that nagging, persistent doubt, the killer might have got away clean.

Rosemary recalled Vera's comment to Desmond the previous day when he'd teased her about Mirella Verratti, the comment where she'd cited all the horrors of the world, all within arm's reach. *War, pestilence, murder, and all manner of duplicity*, she'd said. It had been a portent—one Rosemary should have recognized.

She should have guessed bad luck would follow her—even to the middle of the Atlantic Ocean. Was she destined, somehow, to be always in the wrong place at the wrong time? Or was she really, as Frederick liked to say—and this thought was the one that sent a shiver of fear up her spine—a magnet for murder?

CHAPTER TWELVE

Rosemary exited Dolph's stateroom and decided it was best that, for now, Miss McCoy continue being taken care of by Molly the stewardess, absolving herself of any further obligation, a task she was happy to delay.

She was, however, chomping at the bit to discuss the situation with her friends, so she proceeded to rouse a bleary-eyed Desmond and drag him into the larger suite. Frederick and Vera readied themselves, the adjoining door between the sitting room and bedroom cracked enough to hear Rosemary's explanation.

It didn't take Desmond long to come round, and he regarded her with concern from his perch on a footstool. "Another body, Rose? You really do have the worst luck, don't you?"

"That gets funnier every time I hear it," she replied wryly, tossing him a look that clearly said, *if you can't say anything useful, don't say anything at all*.

Desmond ignored her and asked an even more

infuriating question. "And you're certain it was murder? It couldn't have been an accident of some sort?"

Without giving it even a moment of thought, Rosemary said, "I suppose so if I were willing to chalk a couple of glaring clues up to coincidence and ignore my intuition—which I'm not. Dolph's lamp didn't get wired to that tea tray by accident."

His hands held up in surrender, Desmond seemed to recognize he had wandered into the middle of a hornets' nest and backed off.

"Who do you suppose he could have provoked to the point of wanting him dead?" Frederick wanted to know. "Dolph Sutton was positively the most nondescript man I've ever met—hardly one to make mortal enemies, certainly."

Rosemary cocked her head to one side and reminded the room, "You forget he swapped rooms with his employer. The trap could have been laid before that happened; it could have been meant for Miss McCoy, not Mr. Sutton at all."

Her brother snorted. "Wouldn't that be the rub, eh? To have gone through all that trouble only to do away with the wrong person?" The comment earned him a twin pair of exasperated glances and one nod from Desmond, who seemed to agree with the observation.

Vera sucked in a breath. "In fact, the murderer may yet still be unaware of the swap—of *either* swap," she pointed out, her brow furrowed tightly. "Dolph's room was meant to be yours, Rosie. What if *you* were the intended victim?"

The mood sobered quickly, but Rosemary remained stoic. She had known it was only a matter of time before her friends came to the worrisome conclusion.

"A wire rigged beneath a writing desk simply reeks of a murder mystery, doesn't it? she rationalized. "If you ask me, it's far more likely to have been meant for the author or her secretary."

It was a sound theory and one that appeared to appease Rosemary's traveling companions. After they all declared anyone who tried to hurt her would sorely regret the decision, the discussion returned to one of speculation.

Pacing, Rosemary hypothesized, "The way I see it, there are a few likely possibilities. One, the trap was set before we left Southampton, and the murderer simply walked back off the ship and let the cards fall where they might. In that scenario, both Miss McCoy and I are safe, but a killer walks free, and we never find out who was supposed to die."

Her comment landed like a ton of bricks. Nobody liked that scenario.

"Option number two, the trap was set sometime during the first day of the voyage while we were all exploring the ship. Nobody spent much time below decks that day, leaving plenty of time for the murderer to sneak in and back out unnoticed—especially if they were someone who *belonged* there—either one of the other B2C passengers or staff."

"Surely, the staff members are more likely suspects," Frederick declared. "They have access to all the staterooms and are far more likely to possess the necessary electrical knowledge than most first-class passengers. Opportunity *and* means."

Vera leaned forward, her elbow resting on her crossed knees, and said, "But what about motive? The staff serves countless passengers, and from what I've overheard, they do quite well for themselves in tips. Why risk it? Unless, of course, it was personal."

"Isn't murder always personal?" Rosemary asked. "Someone was made to feel so angry—or jealous, or impotent, perhaps—that they wanted either Miss McCoy or Mr. Sutton dead enough to form a plan and set a trap. This wasn't a moment of rage; it was premeditated, and it absolutely was personal."

"Word travels fast amongst the stewards," Desmond said thoughtfully, "but what if it didn't have to? Stratford certainly knew who was staying in which room, and like Fred said—means and opportunity. I think it would be wise to assume that if he did the deed, Dolph was the intended target."

Rosemary nodded her agreement. "You've hit upon

my third and least desirable theory," she said. "It was Dolph meant to die all along; the murderer succeeded, and their work is done. If that's the case, we might never know the truth."

"Did you tell the captain about your theory?" Vera asked when the ideas began to run dry.

Rosemary shook her head. "I didn't realize until after they'd come for the body. Now, I suppose, I'll have to have a word. He seemed sympathetic; perhaps he'll take me seriously." Her tone indicated she rather doubted the fact, and after a short discussion, it was decided that Desmond would accompany Rosemary to the Enquiry Office up on the Boat Deck, while Vera and Frederick agreed to keep their eyes peeled for any suspicious activity from both passengers and staff.

"Captain Hughes requested we keep news of Dolph's death to ourselves, but frankly, I'm disinclined to," Rosemary said to her brother and Vera. "I rather think you ought to tell everyone in the entire compartment— the Longs, the Parsons, Hattie, everyone. Watch for any out-of-the-ordinary reactions. If the murderer missed his target, you might just witness him realizing his mistake."

"Surely we can wait until after breakfast?" Frederick protested, earning himself a burning look from his sister, who thought the matter a bit more urgent. "Better yet, we deliver the somber news during breakfast," he corrected quickly.

Vera fisted hands on her hips. "Are you daft? No one wants death for breakfast."

Grinning, Frederick grabbed his wife and spun her into his arms. "Death for Breakfast would make a perfect title for the mystery author's second novel, don't you think? We could set ourselves up as her next great muse."

Leave it to Freddie to try and lighten the mood.

Knowing Vera would keep her new husband on his best behavior, Rosemary let Desmond lead her from the suite.

No perusal of the directory posted near the lifts was necessary. Rosemary had taken note of the office's location earlier that morning—a *lot* earlier it seemed, given what had transpired in the short hours between—when her biggest care had been locating the missing piece of her luggage.

She was surprised to discover the term *office* entirely misleading. She had expected a small paneled room with a desk or two and a chair, but it was much more than that. The room was cavernous, with a vaulted ceiling mimicking the one above the Grand Saloon, except on a smaller scale, and dominated in the center by a tall, enclosed circular counter similar to a bank's. Inside, three clerks wove around in an intricate dance, answering questions and otherwise aiding passengers, ensuring the queue moved quickly and efficiently.

Along the outside of the space, against windowed walls that looked out onto the sea, a handful of people milled about or sat in cushioned armchairs, waiting for some form of assistance. Many appeared to merely enjoy the view, which was quite stunning so far above the waterline. Fluffy white clouds reflected off the sea's surface and seemed to stretch to infinity in every direction.

One of the perky clerks approached the counter and called out, "Good morning, sir, madam, how may I help you today?"

"We'd like to speak to Captain Hughes, please. It's about the death in the B Deck suites this morning," Rosemary explained.

The clerk pressed her lips together disapprovingly at the word 'death.' "Oh, I don't know about that," she fluttered, making Rosemary wonder if she wasn't a bit dim. "The captain doesn't take appointments, and of course, he's terribly busy."

It was rare that Rosemary chose to use her social status for personal gain, and nearly every time she did so, it was to help someone other than herself. She pasted a grim smile on her face with that thought in mind.

She looked pointedly at the clerk's name tag. "Miss Addison," Rosemary purred, her voice butter. Desmond glanced at her sideways and took a step back. "Surely the captain can spare a few teeny-tiny moments to speak to one of his *first-class* passengers regarding a *death* in her compartment? I *suppose* I could simply tell all my wealthy friends that Cunard isn't as accommodating as, say, White Star or even the Compagnie Générale Transatlantique!"

Whether it was the perfect French pronunciation or the not-entirely-veiled threat that set the witless Miss Addison to tittering, it wasn't long before Rosemary and Desmond were ushered into the captain's antechamber. To say he looked unimpressed would have been an understatement.

"Mrs. Lillywhite, we meet again, so soon." It didn't sound like a pleasure. "Please, tell me how I can be of service."

Rosemary spared no preamble, for she did understand that Captain Hughes had other important duties to attend to. "Dolph Sutton didn't die from an asthma attack. He was murdered."

If the matter hadn't been so serious, Rosemary might have been tempted to laugh at the incredulous expression on the captain's face. "Whatever do you mean?" he demanded, leading her to wonder which part of her statement had been unclear.

Rosemary explained why she had come to that conclusion, but as she had feared, Captain Hughes remained skeptical. "The doctor examined Mr. Sutton's body himself. He wouldn't have confirmed a cause of death if there was evidence of foul play. What sort of ship do you think I run?" There was a sharpness to the question.

"If she says it's murder, sir, I'm afraid it's true," Desmond retorted.

The captain peered at Rosemary doubtfully and rubbed his chin with his thumb and forefinger. "And what qualifications, precisely, does Mrs. Lillywhite boast to make such a claim?"

Anger flared beneath Rosemary's skin, rising up to pink her cheeks and warm her skin. She seethed silently until she couldn't take it anymore and snapped, "I'm standing right here; perhaps you could speak to me directly."

The captain started, his mouth agape for a fraction of a second before he composed himself and replied so calmly she bristled. "All right then, please answer the question."

"I'd say solving over half a dozen murders counts as qualification enough, wouldn't you?" Rosemary replied coolly but with an effort.

For a moment, Captain Hughes looked as though he might retort in the same manner in which certain types of men always responded to ladies who weren't afraid to speak their minds. But then, with a glance at Desmond and a curious expression, he maintained a semblance of politeness. "I suppose 'qualifications' might have been the wrong word. You have no credentials, certainly, and I can't just take the word of one excitable passenger."

"But I'm not asking you to take my word for it. Go and see for yourself; the electrical wires in the deceased's stateroom were purposely compromised unless there's a legitimate reason why a lamp would be wired to a flattened-out tea tray. You owe it to all your passengers, even the *excitable* ones, to at least ensure their safety before declaring Mr. Sutton's death accidental."

"I don't need to be told how to do my job, Mrs. Lillywhite." There was an edge to the captain's voice now. "It's in the hands of the coroner now. If he finds anything suspicious, we'll certainly follow through, but I suspect it's just as was thought at first glance: accidental death by asphyxiation caused by an asthma attack," said the captain, proving he was indeed abreast of the situation. "I'm very sorry for your loss. It's not easy to accept, but time, as they say, heals all wounds. Now, if you'll excuse me, I have important things to do."

He rubbed his hands together as if wiping them clean and attempted to wave her off, but Rosemary would not be dissuaded. Deep down, she felt that she was right about poor Dolph. She was his only hope for justice, and she refused to be unceremoniously shut down.

Desmond watched her face fall and felt a surge of chivalry course through him. "Now listen here, sir," he

117

began, puffing his chest and arranging his face into a fierce expression.

The captain raised an eyebrow, appearing almost amused until he spoke in a stern tone that brooked no further argument. "No, Mr. Cooper. You listen to me. I'm responsible for all 2,254 passengers aboard this ship, including Mr. Sutton, and it brings me no pleasure to take anyone ashore in a coffin. However, there are systems in place for such occurrences, and if there is any indication of foul play, you can rest assured we'll handle it. Please leave the detective work to the professionals, and please leave my office before I throw you both in the brig. Good day, Mrs. Lillywhite. Mr. Cooper."

When Desmond opened his mouth to argue again, Rosemary tugged on his arm and forced him to follow her out the door. On her way out, she explained her luggage conundrum to Miss Addison, who agreed to swiftly mobilize the stewarding staff for its retrieval.

In the hallway, she explained to Desmond, "There's nothing else we can do except solve the case and prove him wrong. It wouldn't be the first time we were told to mind our own business, would it?"

"No," he replied, "however, you usually at least attempt to stay out of it when pressed by someone like Captain Hughes. I'm all for getting involved, but tell me, what's different this time?"

Without giving the question more than a moment of

thought, Rosemary replied, "I liked him. I've also realized that when it comes to murder, I can't just mind my own business, no matter how hard I try. Somehow, I always manage to find myself in the thick of it anyway, so why resist?"

Desmond didn't have an answer for that question, and neither did Rosemary expect one. "I should have known it wouldn't be as simple as a sail across the Atlantic," she said and left it at that.

Chapter Thirteen

On the way back to her stateroom, Rosemary had knocked lightly on Trix McCoy's door, feeling as though, in some way, the author was her responsibility now. She still had not decided whether that meant she was obligated to reveal her theory regarding Dolph's death, and so when Molly answered her knock and said, "Miss McCoy is still resting, I'm afraid. Perhaps after lunch would be a more appropriate time to visit," Rosemary was secretly relieved for the excuse to put off the emotional task.

Since there was nothing further she could do about the case, she decided to join Vera at the shops. Her friend's insistence that an hour among the fripperies followed by having their hair styled would lift her spirits was not the deciding factor. Rather unfortunately, Rosemary had realized her missing suitcase also carried, in addition to the sport dresses, most of the undergarments Anna had packed for the trip.

Shopping, something Rosemary usually tried to avoid, particularly when Vera was on a tear, was now a necessary task. Rather than sulk about it, she decided to attempt to enjoy herself and, if nothing else, make Vera's day—if only her friend would hurry along and finish readying herself.

"What was wrong with what you wore to breakfast, Vera?" Rosemary asked, just as impatient to leave as were the men.

Frederick let out a guffaw. "I thought you were supposed to be the clever one. Even *I* know better than to ask that question."

"Are you sure we don't need Freddie and Des to join us at the shops?" Rosemary called to Vera after blowing a raspberry at her brother, knowing he and Desmond would rather peel potatoes in the galley all afternoon than stand around watching the two of them model clothing.

When Frederick's expression turned pleading, she took pity and changed the subject. "Speaking of breakfast, how did the rest of the compartment react to Dolph's death? Any clear and obvious murderers make themselves known?"

"Of course not." Frederick dismissed the question. "It couldn't be that easy, could it? Of course, they were all quite sad and asked after Miss McCoy, but none of their heads exploded, and nobody gasped guiltily in horrified

121

shock."

"Perhaps we were on the right track concerning the staff. Why don't you two see what you can dig up?" Rosemary suggested.

The two men needed a task, she decided. They could find trouble in a monastery, which meant an entire luxury ocean liner provided too much distraction—and far too much temptation. Rosemary suspected they would spend more time socializing in one of the lounges or smoking rooms than anything else, anyway.

Her suspicion was confirmed when Frederick picked up the sport jacket lying across the settee and pulled a fat wad of banknotes out of the inside pocket. He tucked them safely into his wallet and winked at Desmond.

It didn't go unnoticed by Vera, who had finally finished dressing and was ready to go. Rosemary appeared to admonish her brother but then snapped her mouth closed. She was no longer Frederick's keeper and never should have had to act as such in the first place. However, he'd made it impossible to trust his judgment was sound—at least until recently. Regardless, now he was Vera's problem!

She, of course, wasn't about to let it go and gasped, "What on earth do you think you're doing, Frederick Woolridge?"

He tossed her a look of confusion and then laughed. "Vera darling, I love you dearly, but as I've said before, unless you've taken a vow of frugality yourself, I'll ask you to kindly mind your own business."

Vera's face turned so red Rosemary thought her head might pop right off her shoulders, but still, she kept her mouth closed, only exchanging a rueful glance with Desmond, who backed away from the center of the stateroom as though it contained a ticking time bomb.

He'd been right and indeed took a shard of verbal shrapnel when Vera declared, "I'm holding you just as responsible, Cooper, and if you drag my husband in over his head, don't think for one second I won't exact revenge—and you know how vindictive I can be."

Desmond did indeed know the length and depth of Vera's wrath; he'd borne its brunt on more than one occasion over the years. Frederick, however, merely quirked a brow, the amused smile never leaving his face. Evidently, he'd become quite unconcerned now that he and Vera were married, but Rosemary felt it rather an unwise decision on his part.

Vera's mouth curled into a grin that could only be described as evil; just like a snake, she was most deadly when she couldn't be seen coming. A flicker of concern crossed Desmond's face, and he took another step back in surrender.

"Relax," Frederick said as if he were speaking to a pair of children, "we're just going to have a little fun, and perhaps—just perhaps—we'll learn something useful to help along your murder investigation."

He kissed a fuming Vera on the cheek and ushered Desmond out, leaving the ladies to their own devices.

'I don't know why I ever fancied myself marrying that man. He's positively insufferable most of the time. Any thought of murder will fly right out of his head the minute someone mentions the stakes of a bet."

Having heard her friend sing a similar refrain on more than one occasion, and since the insufferable man was her brother, Rosemary thought it best to refrain from comment.

"Hmm." She offered a noncommittal sound, then fell silent again as her thoughts returned to death.

"I'm perfectly all right, you know," Rosemary insisted when Vera had glanced at her with a concerned expression for the third time in as many minutes. "It isn't my first dead body."

Vera appeared exasperated. "That's the problem, Rosie—that and, apparently, denial."

"Would you say Max is in denial because he doesn't let the realities of his job turn him into a sobbing mess?" Rosemary wanted to know.

"Of course that's not what I meant," Vera retorted, "but Max is a—"

"A *what*?" Rosemary interrupted when Vera began to stutter. "A man?"

At that, her friend's expression turned from concern to

irritation. "Of course not," she repeated. "I was going to say *a trained professional*. It's not your job to get involved in murder, and I wish you wouldn't. One of these days, one of these hideous investigations will spin out of control, I just know it—and you don't seem worried at all!"

"Since when have you been the type to back down from a challenge? Aren't you the one who usually encourages me to stick my nose in? Honestly, Vera Blackburn Woolridge telling *me* to be careful? Who are you, and what have you done with my friend?"

The joke didn't lighten the mood entirely, but Vera cracked a smile, and Rosemary knew it wouldn't be long now before her friend's joviality was restored. For all her bluster, nothing could keep Vera down for long, not even something as serious as murder.

"Just swear to me, Rosie, that you'll be more careful."

"Of course, I'll be more careful," Rosemary replied, fully intending to follow through on her promise.

CHAPTER FOURTEEN

Up on the Promenade Deck, the shops seemed to call to Vera, and frankly, Rosemary was surprised it had taken her this long to answer. With everything from luggage to jewelry to the latest fashions available—at a premium, of course—there was nothing on display that couldn't be purchased at either end of the voyage. But what was a mere thing like extra money spent when compared to the right to declare that you'd picked up this frock or that watch *en route*?

First up was jewelry, naturally, and while Vera browsed with serious intent, Rosemary interested herself in watching the people milling about. Wealthy couples, businessmen, socialites, and celebrities could all rub shoulders on the Promenade Deck. It was like a scene from one of the society pages, a narrow cross-section of a particular social class that Rosemary had recently begun to realize wasn't representative of the world at large.

Still, the jewelry shop smelled of some exotic flower, reaping the benefits of its location next to the perfumer, and every case sparkled with diamonds, silver, and gold. Even Rosemary had to admit the sight of all that glitter sent a thrill down her spine. "I'd like to see this, this, and this please," Vera said while a pleased-looking clerk pulled pieces out of the case.

Rosemary broke away without Vera noting her absence and wandered over to one of the windows separating the shop interior from the promenade. From her vantage point behind one of the meticulously maintained window displays, Rosemary could see passengers strolling the deck. Some of them even stopped to peer in at the selection of accessories, and one lady went so far as to lean against the glass and cup her hand around her face to shield her eyes from the glare.

With a start, Rosemary realized it was Mrs. Long from the first-class compartment, staring wistfully at a diamond-and-ruby necklace that, by her own admission, was likely well out of her price range. The expression of abject lust painted across the woman's face was enough to convince Rosemary she cared more about money and her station in life than she had claimed to do during breakfast the first morning aboard the ship.

Deftly, Rosemary turned before the other woman could catch sight of her. It would have been equally embarrassing for them both had Mrs. Long noticed Rosemary standing there, staring at her while she stared at the display!

Rosemary rejoined Vera at the counter and dutifully helped sort through potential purchases until a boy—actually, a young man, she realized on further inspection—entered the shop and made a beeline for the case of engagement rings. He began a thorough scan of the pieces on offer and was quickly intercepted by another eager clerk. It seemed, sometimes, as though there were as many staff members as there were passengers to serve.

"Thank you," he said to the clerk and admitted, "I'm quite clueless, truly, when it comes to diamonds. What would you suggest?"

When he looked up, Rosemary felt a pang of sadness. Though the young man bore no physical resemblance to her late husband—where his jaw was soft and round Andrew's had been square and strong—Rosemary recognized in his eyes the same hopeful anticipation that had colored Andrew's face the evening he'd proposed.

It seemed a lifetime ago, and yet, for a moment, she lost herself in a memory so vivid it felt as though she could reach out and touch it. Except she knew the second she tried to grasp it in her hands, the reminiscence would crumble and sift through her fingers like so many grains of sand.

Rosemary sucked in a breath as a pang of grief knocked the wind out of her. Vera had to slap her on the back before she could stop coughing, and by the time she'd righted herself, the young man with the ring was, mercifully, at the other end of the shop paying for his purchase.

"Are you quite all right, Rosie?"

With a nod and a forced smile, Rosemary reassured Vera, keeping her thoughts about Andrew to herself. She felt it was one of life's cruel jokes to let the mind forget about grief even for a moment, only for it to inevitably rush back just as fresh and painful as ever.

"What do you think Freddie will think of this?" Vera asked, pointing to a bauble in the men's section that sent all unpleasant thoughts scuttling back into the dark corners of Rosemary's mind. She stifled a giggle and encouraged her friend, all the while internally rubbing her hands together at the thought of her brother's reaction to Vera's gift. Frederick would positively hate it, and she couldn't wait to see the expression on his face!

While the clerk rang up her purchases, Vera turned to Rosemary and asked, seemingly out of the blue, "Do you think he wants to have a baby?"

For a moment, Rosemary was confused, and then she realized what Vera was asking.

"How should I know? He's your husband; haven't you

129

discussed it?" she asked as they exited onto the central shopping court.

Vera glared a couple of daggers in her direction and said defensively, "Of course, it was all just sort of . . . theoretical, I suppose. You know, distant futures, endless possibilities," she explained, gesticulating with her hands. "We've been happy just to be together, but maybe he isn't as happy as I thought. Maybe he wants more."

"And you don't?" Rosemary wanted to know.

Her friend took a long, deep breath through her nose and opened her mouth to answer when a commotion near the clothing shop caught her attention.

"Looking for Mrs. Verratti!" shouted a steward, loudly enough to be heard clear across the court. "Mrs. Verratti!" A small crowd near the promenade entrance stirred and parted, and then the singer appeared, looking just as chic as ever.

She wore an easy smile and graciously signed an autograph for a beatific admirer while posing for the journalist who never seemed to stray far from her side. His notebook was stowed in favor of just about the most compact camera Rosemary had ever seen. He snapped photos of Mirella Verratti from every angle while admirers pressed closer.

"Why don't you go and say hello?" Rosemary asked Vera, whose longing stare resembled Mrs. Long's from before. She wouldn't have minded asking the journalist for a closer look at that camera. Drawing and painting were one way to create images, photographs quite another, and the thought intrigued her.

Vera shook her head and turned away. "It's pointless. We'd have to shove our way in, and for what? Now isn't the time. Let's go and take care of your undergarment problem," she added, rather more loudly than necessary.

No, Rosemary decided, she did not feel a sense of remorse for setting Vera up to irritate Frederick with her silly gift—none at all!

CHAPTER FIFTEEN

Vera retired to her stateroom following the shopping excursion, leaving Rosemary to speak to Miss McCoy, a task that could be delayed no longer. A light rap on the stateroom door summoned Molly within seconds, and this time Rosemary was told she could step inside.

The stewardess bustled about, fussing over her charge. "Don't overdo it, Miss," she warned gently. "You need your rest now." Out of the author's earshot, Molly warned Rosemary, "Mind, she's taken a number of medications; she may not even understand or remember your conversation."

Rosemary remembered what Frederick had said about the staff—particularly the stewards—having the easiest access to passengers and quickly considered the idea of Molly being involved with the murder.

Electrocution didn't strike her as a particularly feminine crime. In her experience, ladies tended towards poison as a weapon, and as she had just proved, Molly had drugs at her disposal and the knowledge to use them—fatally, if she desired.

Yet, Rosemary couldn't see her having done so. She didn't discount the notion altogether but tucked it away for future contemplation. She'd learned that no potential suspect ought to be counted out entirely, not until the very end, for alibis and motives could be forged or fudged. It wouldn't have been the first time the most unsuspecting of the lot turned out to be a cold-blooded killer!

"I've some things to take care of, Miss," Molly said, interrupting Rosemary's contemplation, "so I'll leave you two to your privacy and return to check on you when I've finished." She received an affectionate and grateful nod from the author in reply.

And then they were alone, Rosemary without any further excuse to delay breaking the bad news. The thought had crossed her mind that it might, in fact, be better if Miss McCoy never found out the truth about her secretary's death. Rosemary couldn't deny that keeping quiet would make things a lot easier for herself. She could simply leave the whole sordid affair alone and carry on with her trip to the States.

Except, doing so went entirely against her nature. The trip—and her sense of moral decency—would be tainted if she simply walked away, and so Rosemary had resigned herself to telling the truth. Whether the author could handle it didn't matter much; she deserved to know what had happened to Mr. Sutton.

"I'm terribly sorry, again, for your loss, Miss McCoy. How are you feeling?" Rosemary said, taking a seat on the chair pulled over to the side of the bed. It felt incredibly intimate to see her this way, yet neither of the women seemed particularly bothered. They had shared an even more unsettling encounter earlier, though it felt like far longer ago than mere hours.

"I think we're more than acquaintances now, don't you, Rosemary?" the author replied, using her given name as if she'd read Rosemary's mind. The trace of bitterness in her voice indicated she might have preferred they remain strangers under the circumstances.

When Rosemary agreed, Miss McCoy answered her first question. "I'm feeling about as well as could be expected. It'd be better if the sedatives would only take effect. I would love nothing more than to fall asleep and wake up having already docked, but alas, those pills don't seem to be working." There was a long silence, and then she said, "I still can't believe he's gone."

Rosemary looked into the other woman's eyes, took a deep breath, and trod into murky waters. "I don't quite know how to tell you this, Trix, but I've had some experience in these matters, and I'm afraid I don't think Dolph died of natural causes. I believe he was murdered."

The author looked as though she might burst into laughter or tears, her eyebrows lost beneath the fringe that covered her forehead. "I—I—what? Who?" Miss McCoy stuttered through the beginning of several questions before settling on, "How could you possibly know that?"

A short explanation of how Rosemary had discovered the miswired lamp and noticed the mark on Dolph's foot ensued, along with a description of the captain's reaction and what she considered a denial of the facts. She expected Miss McCoy to burst into tears or begin an emotional landslide, but instead, she said, albeit an octave above her usual voice, "Wouldn't he be tickled by the irony?"

Rosemary supposed it *was* somewhat ironic for the secretary of a murder mystery author to have been murdered, but more so than that, it was coincidental— too coincidental for her liking.

"Who aboard this ship would have wanted Dolph dead? Did he have enemies or know anyone else on board?" The questions tumbled out of her mouth almost involuntarily. "Perhaps one of the stewards or other staff members? He spoke as though he was a frequent traveler."

"You don't honestly believe Dolph was the intended target, do you?" Miss McCoy peered at Rosemary as if she were daft, and Rosemary thought it fortuitous for her that the author had just suffered a loss. However, the next person who acted as though she had nothing but fluff between her ears would receive a rare Lillywhite tongue-lashing—just not a grieving woman. Rosemary wasn't a monster, after all.

Instead, she pretended the question had been asked with some politeness and replied, "Frankly, I wish I did believe that. Then I might not be worried about your safety—or my own. Dolph's room was meant to be mine if you recall."

The last bit caused Trix's eyes to widen in doubt and disbelief. "Whoever would want to kill you?"

Rosemary reminded herself again that Miss McCoy had suffered a terrible loss and that patience was a virtue. "The list is longer than you might expect," she replied.

Miss McCoy still appeared doubtful. "No," she said, and her gaze shifted to something in the distance only she could see. "It's my celebrity that killed him. Dolph's death is on my conscience. It was probably a crazed fan. There's no other explanation."

It seemed to Rosemary there were many other explanations, but she could see that Miss McCoy was in shock. She suspected the medication Molly had administered before her arrival had finally begun to take effect, and what came out of Trix's mouth next did nothing to quell the notion.

"That young lady Miss Humphries asked an awful lot of prying questions about my book. Perhaps she's responsible for Dolph's missing notebook as well."

Hattie was one of the last people Rosemary would have expected the author to incriminate, though she had to admit that in a murder mystery novel, the ingenuous young lady traveling alone in first class would have been a tempting suspect. Rosemary had interpreted her keenness to cozy up to Trix as the action of an enthusiastic fan, and though she couldn't deny the possibility that Hattie might well be responsible for the missing notebook containing the author's next bestseller, branding her a murderer felt somewhat premature.

"Poor Dolph," Miss McCoy went on, her eyes taking on that faraway expression once again. "He wouldn't have hurt a fly—literally. I've seen him catch spiders and carry them safely outdoors. It shouldn't be him lying in that coffin below decks. It should be me!"

If, like her brother, Rosemary had been interested in high-stakes wagering, she would have laid money on the fact that Trix McCoy had cared deeply for Randolph Sutton and gravely regretted his death. And yet, she couldn't ignore the glaringly obvious fact that the author herself was a prime suspect—a more likely one than Hattie, to be sure.

After all, besides his employer, who had had any relationship with Dolph?

Rosemary had witnessed the pair interact enough to know they shared a bond beyond a casual working relationship. She believed genuine affection had existed between them—but that didn't mean Trix had no reason to want him dead. In fact, that familiarity was what, to Rosemary's mind, propelled her to the top of the list.

If experience had taught Rosemary anything, it was that murder was an act rarely committed in the absence of emotion. She had seen many struck down over hate and even more over love—but none due to indifference. That made Trix McCoy a person of interest, and whether Rosemary believed her guilty or not, she simply couldn't turn a blind eye to the facts.

She couldn't continue forcing the lady to talk when she was clearly in distress. Surreptitiously, Rosemary rang the bell for the stewardess. Mercifully, Molly returned quickly, looking slightly the worse for wear, and shooed her out of the room, assuring, "I'll see to Miss McCoy, don't you worry. She needs to rest." With that, Rosemary wholeheartedly agreed and made a grateful escape.

In the hall, she shut the author's stateroom door and leaned her head against it. After a couple of deep, cleansing breaths, Rosemary turned to discover none other than Hattie herself standing near the threshold to the common area, carrying a book and wearing an enigmatic expression. When their eyes met, the girl's mouth turned into a sympathetic smile.

She seemed to make up her mind and approached Rosemary asking, "How is she? We've all heard what happened to poor Mr. Sutton. What a shame. I'm sure it was a frightful experience, finding him that way."

The expression on her face told Rosemary Hattie knew she'd been there when Dolph's body was found, and Miss McCoy's accusation echoed in her ear. She regarded Hattie with suspicion for a moment, but then she remembered Frederick and Vera had informed all the passengers in the compartment of her involvement over breakfast.

As quickly as it had arrived, Rosemary shook off the absurd notion and accepted Hattie's words of regret. "Truly, it is. I'm sure Miss McCoy would appreciate your condolences, but perhaps not just now. She's resting."

And, she thinks you're the one who killed him, Rosemary added silently, *so it's unlikely you'd receive a warm welcome*. She declined to mention anything about foul play; better to let whoever *did* kill Dolph think they'd got away with it free and clear. Whether Hattie was guilty or not, Rosemary doubted she'd keep any bit of inside information to herself.

The young lady seemed disappointed at the dismissal and eager to hear more about Dolph's death, so much so that she practically followed Rosemary into her stateroom. Deftly, Rosemary sidestepped her attempts to pry and shut the door in her face with a promise to "have a chat sometime later in the evening"—an empty promise she'd no intention of keeping!

Chapter Sixteen

When Rosemary gained the quiet sanctuary of her stateroom, she discovered that, somehow, Miss Addison from the Enquiry Office had managed to organize the retrieval of her missing suitcase. The uncharitable thought that she still probably wasn't any less daft than she'd appeared to be crossed Rosemary's mind, and she didn't even immediately regret it.

Any joy this news might have wrought got canceled out by the morning's ordeal, which had put Rosemary in a really foul mood. What had Dolph done to get himself killed? Or alternatively, what had Trix McCoy done to make herself a target? Could it simply be, just as the author suspected, a case of a crazed fan? That sort of thing had been known to happen. People committed murder for all sorts of reasons, but this one seemed far-fetched, particularly given Miss McCoy wasn't what Rosemary would consider a celebrity.

Had either half of the Verratti couple turned up dead,

Rosemary wouldn't have batted an eyelid at the notion. If a crazed fan were to strike aboard the ship, one of them would certainly be the target, rather than a woman who merely penned mystery novels. And yet, if one were thinking poetically, wouldn't a murder mystery author be the perfect target?

Rosemary took a deep breath and forced her mind to quiet, to search for something—anything—besides Dolph's murder upon which to focus. Her gaze returned to the recently delivered suitcase, and she was grateful for the mundane task. She reached for the handle just as someone knocked on the door.

"It's me." Vera's voice only preceded her face by a mere second. "Frederick sent me to check on you."

While his brotherly concern might be touching under other circumstances, it did nothing to mitigate Rosemary's current mood. "Tell him I've yet to succumb to a fit of the vapors. Nor have I descended into trauma-induced madness."

When Vera arched a brow, Rosemary apologized and made an effort to let go of the pall murder had cast over her day.

"At least my missing case has arrived." Grasping the handle, Rosemary was taken aback when she found it much heavier than expected.

Hadn't she watched Wadsworth stack this case, easily, on top of the pyramid of luggage bearing her stripe of cream and maroon? He had picked it up and tossed it there like it weighed nothing, which it practically did since it had only been filled with the gauzy crepe de Chine sport dresses and a collection of undergarments. Wadsworth was stronger than he looked at first glance and more formidable besides, but he was no bodybuilder.

Rosemary laid the suitcase on the bed with a furrowed brow and flipped open the latches. "What in the world?" She slammed the lid back closed, her breath a gasp, and then opened it again. What was inside sparkled in the glow of the bedside lamp, and for a moment, Rosemary imagined she was a character in Robert Louis Stevenson's famous novel—riding the high seas, hunting treasure, and fighting pirates!

The diamond-encrusted necklace and tiara looked like something out of the British Museum, and though it wasn't a cache of gold doubloons, the stack of cash still constituted a treasure by every definition of the word. She might not have possessed the ability to tell an authentic diamond from a facsimile at fifty paces, but Rosemary certainly didn't need a jeweler's loupe to know what was in the case was the real thing.

And to think she'd worried the biggest problem with her luggage would be having something stolen, not finding something far more valuable than anything she had brought on board!

"What?" When Vera crowded in for a look, her eyes didn't widen in surprise, and she didn't gasp. She merely raised one eyebrow and let out a low whistle at the sight of the shimmering jewels and a stack of American banknotes.

"Whatever are you doing with a thousand pounds worth of diamonds?" she asked archly.

Taken aback, Rosemary gaped. *"That's* how much they're worth? How do you know that?"

With a roll of her eyes, Vera dismissed the question. "That's at least fifteen carats of exquisitely cut stones, some of them quite large on their own. The tiara isn't as extravagant—those are very tiny gems—though just as beautiful in my opinion because the effect is quite stunning. Still, we're looking at a fortune in jewels and," Vera picked up the stack of money, thumbed through it too quickly to have had time for a thorough tally, "somewhere around five hundred American dollars."

"Have you been leading some life of crime I'm unaware of? Does Freddie know you can estimate the worth of diamonds and banknotes with a mere look?" Rosemary joked.

Vera widened and then batted her eyes, feigning a coy expression. "Any lady worth her salt must strive to carry an air of mystery. That's one of Lorraine's rules of proper comportment. Number seven, if I remember correctly."

"Lorraine is definitely not a follower of Emily Post." The last of Rosemary's bad mood evaporated at the mention of Vera's mother, who lived life on her own terms and expected her daughter to do the same. "Nevertheless, this is not my case."

Sighing, Vera picked up the tiara and went to the mirror to try it on. "Of course it isn't. Even so, this looks fabulous on me, don't you think?"

"I think it's exquisite and would look fabulous wrapped around a warthog, but yes, you're always the most dazzling thing in the room."

"Are you stroking my vanity again?" Vera preened and ignored Rosemary's long-suffering expression.

Now that the shock had worn off, Rosemary inspected the suitcase more fully. The interior was a creamy-yellow color and not the royal-blue that lined her own luggage. In addition to money and jewels, the case held a bottle of rum and a trinket box which, when opened, revealed a lapel pin with a ship's insignia on it, similar to those worn by the staff and captain.

She closed the lid again gently and looked more closely at the band. This case was striped with the same color pattern as her own, but the section of maroon was a tiny bit thicker.

"This case is quite similar to mine. I can see how the steward might make such a mistake," Rosemary said. She reached into the pocket of the top portion in hopes of discovering some clue to the owner's identity, only to find a map of the London underground and a novel that looked as if it had never been read.

Her brow furrowed when she realized it was a copy of none other than Trix McCoy's mystery, *Mrs. Willoughby and the Poisoned Pen.*

She handed her find to Vera, who said, "Do you think this case belongs to Miss McCoy?"

Rosemary rejected the idea immediately. "It's a popular novel. There must be dozens of copies in suitcases all over the ship. Besides, Miss McCoy doesn't seem like the type to be carrying such lavish, expensive jewelry, and if she were, I don't think she'd throw it around higgledy-piggledy."

Success had come to the lady quickly, and she struck Rosemary as what her mother would call *nouveau riche*. She might throw her wealth around to purchase a piece of lavish jewelry, but she wouldn't literally throw the diamonds, loose, into a suitcase.

Despite the curious lapel pin there was little doubt in Rosemary's mind the owner of the case was traveling on a first-class ticket. It made sense that the steward had found this piece of luggage somewhere within the same area as the rest of her own trunks—the first-class cargo hold below decks. Perhaps whoever owned it was wealthy enough that to them, its contents constituted mere baubles—what a thought! Why else wouldn't they have simply stored them in the purser's safe-deposit box?

And then Rosemary thought of something—perhaps her first fanciful notion hadn't been far off. Perhaps Miss McCoy's smuggling plot wasn't so outlandish after all! Could the jewels have been stolen and were now being smuggled into America to be sold off to the highest bidder?

Even if that were true, the case and its contents weren't hers, and she had little confidence about handing it over to the steward who had erroneously delivered it in the first place. If, as Frederick and Desmond had suggested, the stewards were stealing from the passengers, they weren't doing a very good job if they'd overlooked such a fortune.

Vera replaced the tiara with an even deeper sigh, her fingers giving it one final caress. "Shall we call the steward back? Or would you like me to accompany you to the Enquiry Office?"

"There's no need, but I confess I would feel better about the situation if I could see the suitcase returned to its rightful owner. The next person who finds it might not be as scrupulous as me." The decision had nothing to do with curiosity about who the thing belonged to, Rosemary told herself, nothing whatsoever.

"If you're certain, I should go and get ready for dinner. You will be joining us, won't you? I'd hate to think of you sitting here alone."

"I will, and I am quite all right, you know. This isn't my first murder, after all."

Rosemary saw Vera to the door and then, with a sigh of resignation, picked up the heavy case and prepared to return to the Boat Deck, hoping Captain Hughes would be otherwise engaged. She dared not risk another encounter with *him*, given their mutual displeasure following the first.

On her way through the common room towards the lift, Rosemary noticed Frederick playing a spirited chess game with young Stewart Long. Her brother appeared quite jovial, which was his default, and she recognized the fond expression he wore when interacting with their sister's boy, Nelly.

Perhaps Vera was right about his desire to start a family. As she continued to the lift, Rosemary decided the two of them would have to work it out on their own. She was quite content, again, to stay out of their business. However, whether they would allow her to do so was another matter.

"Need some help with that, Rosie?" Frederick called from across the room. She thanked him but waved him off, though she was relieved to find the corridor deserted and the lift waiting empty, as if especially for her.

"Which floor, madam?" the operator asked, but when Rosemary opened her mouth to tell him she needed the

Boat Deck, the words died on her lips.

The thought of having to return to the Enquiry Office, chance running into Captain Hughes, and try to explain her quandary to Miss Addison made her cringe internally. Wouldn't the clerk simply call down to the stewards' bureau anyway?

She made an impulsive decision, one she would reflect upon later with mixed emotions, and asked the attendant to take her just one level down to C Deck straightaway.

Chapter Seventeen

Rosemary exited the lift and took a moment to get her bearings. Forward would lead her to the top of the grand staircase, overlooking the first-class dining saloon, but instead, she walked aft towards the ship's midsection where guest services—configured to resemble the shopping court two levels above—acted as a separator between first and second classes.

On the port side, the barbershop and hairdresser flanked the laundry service, their window displays filled with models of all the latest hairstyles. Opposite and starboard, the purser's desk and stewards' bureau shared space with the correspondence station where one could send or receive a telegram at all hours of the day and night.

"Can I assist you, madam?" the clerk manning the purser's desk asked politely, just as his counterpart on the stewards' side turned away to return a tagged key to the rack mounted on the wall. Each little hook bore a label, and she noted idly that the stewards did indeed seem to have access to every nook and cranny of the ship.

Rosemary looked between the purser and steward and made another quick decision. She ducked inside and, after a short few minutes, emerged, significantly lighter in the absence of both the case itself and the anxiety she felt carrying it around and knowing what was inside.

A spring in her step, Rosemary was poised to turn left back towards the first-class staircase when she caught the sound of jazz music emanating from the opposite direction. It was a jaunty tune that, even in snippets, made her think of drinks and dancing in the nightclubs of London. Curious, she changed course and headed further aft towards the second-class entrance—a place she, as a first-class passenger, was quite forbidden to enter.

A little thrill ran through her. Impulsively, Rosemary glanced around, noted that none of the few nearby passengers were paying her any attention, and slipped through the corridor, down another hallway, and finally arrived in front of the second-class staircase. While less lavish than the one leading to the Grand Saloon, it was still quite impressive, its banisters carved in a similar but simpler style.

Louder now, the music called to her like a siren's song, further piquing her curiosity and propelling her forward almost involuntarily. Rosemary wandered a bit further and peeked into the second-class lounge.

Her first impression was of dark-paneled walls with slightly less ornate trim than that in the first-class one. Also on the plainer side, the tables and chairs were still of good quality and looked comfortable.

A cheerful buzz of conversation and laughter competed with the sprightly song that had served to draw her there. Passengers danced, played games, or just lounged and chatted. The whole room carried a more relaxed atmosphere as people appeared less concerned with maintaining a level of social status than with just enjoying the voyage.

Rosemary longed to stay for another tune but knew she was pushing her luck just by being there. She turned around reluctantly and retraced her steps back towards the second-class entrance to discover Molly, the stewardess, loitering near the lift in a perfect position to see her coming out of an area where they both knew she didn't belong.

It didn't occur to her that there likely wouldn't be much of a fuss made over a lady from the upper decks trespassing on a lower one, and she panicked at the sight of the stewardess, retreating in the direction of the second-class entrance.

Rosemary was trapped. She couldn't loiter there, nor could she risk being caught reentering the common area from the wrong direction with Molly standing right there, so she chose the only other option and took the stairs down even further into the bowels of the ship.

She was much further aft than usual, in an unfamiliar stairwell, and when she arrived on D Deck found herself near the kitchens amid a hubbub of dinner preparation. With no clear path to safety, Rosemary cursed her inquisitive nature, wishing she'd simply waited for the lift instead of following her curiosity.

She ducked back out of the kitchens and picked up her pace, skipping the E Deck which, she recalled, was home to the stewards' accommodations, and arrived on the deserted F level, quite breathless.

Again, Rosemary consulted the posted directory and was relieved to discover she could simply cut through the Turkish baths and pick up the lift to her compartment on the fore-end of the ship. Her shoulders sagged with relief. She'd only wanted to sate her curiosity, not tour the entire vessel.

And yet, when her eye caught the words "first-class cargo hold," Rosemary decided one more flight wouldn't kill her! If the staff couldn't find her missing case, perhaps she could find it herself.

Down the stairs she went, expecting to be able to continue forward unobstructed and discovering that on the lower decks, there were far fewer open spaces than up top. Rosemary snaked her way through a maze of dry-food storage until, finally, she neared her destination.

All the excitement drained out of her when she heard a gruff voice and stilled, peering around the corner to see two formidable-looking men standing in front of the first-class cargo hold entrance.

The bigger, more brutish one leaned against the wall. "Jimmy, if we don't find that case, the boss will have our hide, you know that, right?" he said in a thick American accent.

His companion, a wiry man with a squeaky voice, replied, "I ain't nobody's patsy," and knelt down in front of the door. Rosemary dove back behind the wall, wanting desperately to avoid being seen. She could hear a scraping sound and then a jingle and concluded they were attempting to pick the lock.

"No way I'm doing time for this job," Jimmy continued. "I say we find it, take the diamonds for ourselves. Come on, Tony, let's do it."

Rosemary's breath caught in her throat at the mention of diamonds, and she realized with a start she knew exactly which ones—and which case—they meant. If they were after it, Jimmy and Tony were dangerous.

The promise she'd made to Vera was still fresh on her lips, and here she was putting herself in harm's way yet again. She was stuck for however long it took the pair to either succeed in opening the door or give up trying.

Rosemary took a chance at being spotted to peek around the corner, holding her breath as she watched and listened.

"And then what? Where would we go?" the one named Tony replied. "Even if we made it off this floating wreck without getting caught, we'd have to leave town for good."

"You mean like go to Jersey?"

Tony grunted. "No, Jimmy, not to Jersey. What, you got nobody home in there?" He knocked his knuckles against Jimmy's forehead. "Jersey ain't gonna be far enough."

"What about Chicago? I got a cousin in Chicago. Says it's real windy." Jimmy laughed at his own joke until Tony slugged him harder than before.

"We cross the boss, and Chicago ain't gonna be far enough either. Hell, San Francisco ain't gonna be far enough. We cross the boss, and it's gonna be *us* in those coffins. Now, let's find the damn case, get the diamonds back, and get done with this job before it gets done with us. It ain't worth it, Jimmy. If I'm lyin', I'm dyin'."

The mention of San Francisco seemed to sober Jimmy enough to render him speechless, and after a few moments, Rosemary realized the pair had managed to get the door open and were now inside the cargo hold.

She let out the breath she'd been holding in and thought about what she'd overheard. Someone was looking for the suitcase that had been delivered to her stateroom. Truly, the realization came as no shock; Rosemary had been concerned with her own lost luggage and what hers carried was far less valuable.

What on earth had she gotten herself mixed up in? Who was the boss? And had Dolph somehow got himself caught in his crosshairs?

Relieved to be spared what would surely have been an unpleasant encounter, Rosemary vowed to consider the possibilities once out of harm's way and made her escape, up the stairs two at a time. She knew they wouldn't find what they were looking for in there because the case was safe and sound inside the purser's safety deposit box, and she was the one with the key!

Chapter Eighteen

After several flights, all the adrenaline coursing through Rosemary's system had been spent, and also, she had no idea which level she was on. Evidently, the staff routes worked differently than those designated for passengers and were less clearly marked. Though she was sure she'd climbed high enough to be back in the first-class section, every door led to an unfamiliar corridor.

She was even more grateful she wasn't still carrying the heavy suitcase. It was safe, for the time being, until she could decide what to do with it.

Finally, after what felt like hours and thousands of steps, Rosemary emerged in a corridor that was most definitely part of the ship's first-class area. In fact, it was even more opulent here than in her own compartment, and that was when Rosemary realized she was, for the third time in an hour, in a part of the ship where she didn't belong: the very exclusive, very private

Millionaires' Suites!

Even though she had flouted rules before, being discovered snooping around here would constitute an embarrassment she wasn't sure Vera would ever forgive. As if the thought of her friend had summoned the famous singer she so idolized, Rosemary heard the dulcet tones of Mirella Verratti's emotion-infused voice as it drifted out of a partially open door into the hallway.

"How much higher a pedestal could you possibly require?" her husband replied. His voice was velvet, peach fuzz, and champagne bubbles, but his words were the edge of a knife. "The entire world adores you."

"And what's wrong with being dedicated to my career? It's my passion!" she fired back, her tone an example of the very thing she defended.

Mr. Verratti practically shouted, "Because you belong to your fans, Mirella, to the masses and the press. Not to me—never to me! I cannot compete with them, and I don't wish to try anymore."

Brows raised over wide eyes, Rosemary forgot that she was somewhere she was not supposed to be. Curiosity trumped self-preservation, and after all, what could they really do to her? Throw her in the brig for making a mistake?

"The public does not control me. Nor do you." Mirella's voice held a wealth of scorn. "Jealousy is a most unattractive trait in a man."

Mr. Verratti raised his. "Call me ugly if you must, but I will not be the second fiddle in your orchestra. It's over!"

Rosemary's mouth had fallen open in shock. She couldn't reconcile the love she'd seen between this man and this woman to the words she heard coming from them now. Surely a husband and wife wouldn't turn on each other so quickly? Unless the confines of an ocean liner put them in too close a proximity, which Rosemary was willing to admit could be a problem. She, herself, had begun to feel penned in with fewer opportunities for solitude. If the noise and motion were taking their toll on her, how much worse could it be for a couple already dealing with the stress of being in the spotlight?

When she spoke again, Mrs. Verratti sounded smaller somehow, as though she'd moved to the other side of the room, or perhaps she had simply been hit over the head with a painful truth she hadn't been ready to face.

"Very well. If that's what you want, then that's what you shall get."

Unable to bear the misery in the woman's voice—or to justify eavesdropping any longer—Rosemary crept away down the hall. Finally, she reached the first-class lifts and felt an overwhelming sense of relief. Her muscles ached from running up and down the stairs, and a layer of sweat and grime had accumulated on her skin. She yearned for a nice long soak in a scalding bath and decided to forgo the formal dinner. Spending the remainder of the evening tucked into bed with a book sounded like just the thing.

Vera was there, waiting, dressed to the nines, when she arrived at her room. In the time it had taken for Rosemary to run the ship from hull to mast, her friend had only succeeded in dressing for dinner! "Oh, you're here," Rosemary said, a trace of disappointment coloring her voice.

"Lovely to see you, too, Rosie," Vera replied, affecting a crestfallen expression and sulky tone. "Are you quite all right? You haven't found another body, have you?" Now, she sounded positively eager.

"No, of course not," Rosemary retorted, although she had to admit it was a valid question. "And I'm not unhappy to see you; it's just that I've something to tell you—something I overheard—and I know that you're going to overreact when I do."

Vera's eyebrows shot into her hairline. "What is it? Is it Frederick? Did he and Desmond get themselves in over their heads again? Lose a load of money on another ludicrous bet?"

Rosemary grimaced and shook her head. "No, nothing like that. It's not about Freddie. It's about the Verrattis."

"Oh no! What is it?" Vera appeared more concerned at the mention of the celebrity couple than she had been about her husband, but Rosemary knew that had more to do with an abundance of faith in Frederick rather than a lack thereof and only made her feel worse for having to break the news.

"It seems their marriage is over." Rosemary relayed the conversation she had overheard, repeating every line she could remember several times and reassuring her friend she was certain she hadn't forgotten anything important.

Vera sank down on an armchair and sighed. "Mirella and Gianni heading for the divorce court! I can hardly believe it. You're certain?" she asked one more time for good measure.

"A shame, I agree, but perhaps they're simply not meant for one another," Rosemary speculated to Vera's sudden amusement.

"Don't let your mother hear you advocate divorce," she chided. "She'll have you chained up in the cellar of the ladies' auxiliary hall, being doused with holy water and read scripture out of *Etiquette* until you've mended your wanton ways!"

It was an interesting visual and not all that difficult for Rosemary to picture. Evelyn Woolridge could give Emily Post a run for her money on the subject of proper decorum.

Rosemary shrugged. "My mother sees the world in black and white; right or wrong; polite and unseemly. Perhaps it's her generation, but you and I both know the world is nothing but shades of grey. Unfortunately, it seems that more often than not, it's the women who are forced to put up with all sorts of abuses with no way out! We take many vows during a wedding, yet the only part expected to be upheld is the 'until death do us part' part. What about the rest of it—the love, honor, and cherish?"

Vera held her hands up in surrender. "It's not me who needs convincing. Perhaps you're right. Perhaps there's more simmering beneath the surface of the Verrattis' marriage than the public sees. I think I'll just keep an eye on them. If nothing else, it's bound to be more intriguing than any of the other gossip on board this ship. Now that I'm married, I've little patience for the tournament-style husband hunt that's in full swing on the Promenade Deck."

Vera stopped talking, tilted her head to one side, peering at her friend, and then said, "What did you do, spend the last hour in the gymnasium? You look dreadful, Rosie."

"Why, thank you ever so much," came Rosemary's dry reply.

Vera ignored the comment and said, "You certainly can't go to dinner like that. Why don't you just get into bed and let me call down for a dinner tray? I think it's been rather a long day for you, hasn't it?"

Gratefully, Rosemary accepted the suggestion. "It has, and you don't even know the half of it. Now, about that dinner tray—it's going to need to include a double shot of gin, and you might as well make one for yourself because you're not going to believe this . . ."

Chapter Nineteen

Even exhausted, Rosemary was unable to put down *Mrs. Willoughby and the Poisoned Pen* and stayed up most of the night to finish it. She could see why it was such a sensation with murder mystery fans; a seasoned lady detective, even she had been kept guessing who had done it until the very end!

Rosemary supposed she ought not to have been surprised; it stood to reason the novel deserved its praise, and Trix as well for having written it. And yet, she hadn't expected to thoroughly enjoy the plot—and also the story, for one was not to be confused with the other, according to the author herself.

There was more to Miss McCoy than met the eye. Any woman shrewd enough to have written a book with as many twists and turns as the *Poisoned Pen* knew more than she claimed to regarding the murder of her own secretary, of that Rosemary was certain. Proof of her ingenuity was also proof she could have committed the murder herself, for that matter.

Trix McCoy had woven a tale of murder and intrigue, and now, by a twist of fate, Rosemary had become embroiled in a mystery just like something out of a novel: a seemingly accidental death, an array of potential suspects served on a silver platter, and a race against time to bring the killer to justice! It was a plot with which she was already all too familiar, and it did cause some concern to realize how closely she identified with the main character.

Just like Mrs. Willoughby, Rosemary was up against a circular problem; did Trix kill Dolph Sutton, or was she the real murderer's true target? Or did it all have to do with the mysterious suitcase full of jewels and the big bad boss mentioned by Jimmy and Tony?

Rosemary was disappointed when the author sat down at the other end of the table and barely spoke. Miss McCoy pushed a poached egg around her plate and drained a cup of soot-black coffee to the dregs without saying a word. Despite her reluctance to discuss Dolph's death, it didn't take long for the conversation to arrive there on its own.

"I'm very sorry for your loss," Hattie Humphries said sympathetically, the sentiment immediately echoed by both of the Longs. It then made its way around the table with less and less fervor until, finally, Mr. Tait merely sent a sympathetic frown in her direction and resumed his perusal of the *The Atlantic Edition*.

The author paled. "Thank you all," she said, her voice strained, "but I have an appointment with the ship's doctor, and I shouldn't think he'd appreciate lateness. Good day." She hurried towards the exit faster than Rosemary had ever seen her move, as though she couldn't get away from the table quickly enough.

Only pondering her decision for a split second, Rosemary followed. "Trix, wait," she said, catching up to her near the lift. "Are you sure you're quite all right?"

The author turned and replied stiffly, all the informality of the previous day having evaporated along with the sliver of emotion she had displayed at the breakfast table. Her face was now the same stony mask Rosemary had seen her wear the previous morning after Captain Hughes' insensitive remark.

"Of course, Mrs. Lillywhite," the author replied. "Why wouldn't I be? Tragedies strike every day, don't they? I certainly don't hold a monopoly on grief."

From the depths of her memory, Rosemary recalled having felt the same way in the wake of her husband's death. Hating to see anyone hurting, she said sincerely, "I'd like to offer my condolences once more and also my investigative services. I quite liked Mr. Sutton, and I want to see his killer brought to justice."

Miss McCoy raised a hand. "There's no need. Please, Mrs. Lillywhite, I appreciated your kindness during a difficult time yesterday, but this idea that Dolph was murdered—it's absurd! He was a good man who took enough abuse during his life; I won't have you sullying his memory."

Bewildered, Rosemary gaped at the author. The day before, she had believed it possible, had accepted the idea that she herself might have been a target. Of course, Miss McCoy had also been administered some powerful sedatives prior to the conversation, so perhaps she hadn't been as lucid as she'd seemed.

"But, how do you explain the lamp and the tea tray?"

"I've spoken to Captain Hughes," Miss McCoy revealed after a pregnant pause, "and he's assured me Dolph's stateroom was thoroughly searched yesterday evening and found to be in tip-top shape. In fact, there was nothing wrong with his desk lamp at all. Whatever it is you're playing at, leave me out of it. I've suffered enough."

When Rosemary opened her mouth to defend herself, Miss McCoy cut her off with a resolute, "Good day, Mrs. Lillywhite," and stalked away.

Bewildered, Rosemary stared at the author's retreating back. Not for one second did she think Captain Hughes, no matter how cantankerous or disbelieving, would cover up a murder on his own ship, and that could only mean one thing: someone else, most likely the killer, removed all evidence of the crime sometime between the discovery of the body the morning before, and that evening when the captain's men performed their search.

She knew for sure she'd left the key with Trix after tidying Dolph's stateroom, which meant the author could have used it to reenter and dispose of the evidence. It didn't fit with her impression of their relationship, but hadn't she been the one to point out that people didn't generally commit murder over indifference?

There could have been, Rosemary rationalized, a deeper connection between the pair, a private connection, perhaps, or an unrequited love? Trix could have been rejected and lashed out, but if that were the case, she would have expected something like a blow to the head rather than a premeditated electrocution trap.

Something about the scenario simply didn't fit together. What Rosemary did know was that it wouldn't have been difficult for a determined individual to pick Dolph's stateroom door lock—she knew two unscrupulous fellows who already possessed the required accoutrements to pull it off. She found it far more likely Dolph had found himself, perhaps even accidentally, involved in whatever scheme had prompted Jimmy and Tony to break into the cargo hold.

When Rosemary returned to the table, it was to find Frederick, quite incapable of maintaining any sense of discretion, talking animatedly with the rest of the group.

Vera smiled apologetically in his defense, and Rosemary knew there was nothing she could have done to stop him.

"What happened, exactly, to Mr. Sutton?" Hattie asked unabashedly, her eyes bright with macabre curiosity. "Was it gruesome?"

Rosemary shook her head. "I see my brother has informed you all of my role in the discovery of Mr. Sutton's death. To answer your question, Hattie, no, it was not gruesome. Not at all. He might have been sleeping—to have simply slipped away. That was a relief. I've certainly seen worse."

Mr. Tait started and stared at Rosemary. "Whatever do you mean?" he asked.

She tried to think of a way to cover the slip, cursing Frederick for his contagious verbal incontinence, but before she could open her mouth to smooth over the situation, Desmond piped up helpfully, "Mr. Tait, our Rosie here is better than any top-notch London detective!"

"Thank you, Des," she retorted sharply. "I hope I shall have learned enough in the course of my investigations to get away with *your* murder."

"Really?" Hattie leaned forward, dropping her toast back onto her plate and staring at Rosemary with renewed interest. "You're a real-life lady sleuth? Just like a character in a mystery novel? Just like Mrs.

Willoughby?"

With withering glares directed toward her friends, Rosemary capitulated slightly. "Mrs. Willoughby is eighty-two, so perhaps not *just* like; not all widows are octogenarians, you know. And, of course, I'm a living person and not a character in a book. I've contributed to the resolution of a couple of local murders, that's all. Truly, nothing terribly interesting, isn't that right, Desmond?" She tried to kick him underneath the table, but he was astute enough to move his leg out of her reach.

To add insult to injury, Frederick couldn't seem to stop himself. "You caught the killer who murdered a mass murderer," he exclaimed. "How much more interesting can you get, Rosie?"

Mr. Tait stroked his beard thoughtfully. "So you've been involved in more than one case of murder, and then a death just happened to occur in your corridor? Seems an interesting coincidence," he mused, leaning back in his chair and eyeing Rosemary speculatively.

"Please," Rosemary said, stopping him, "do not call me a magnet for murder. I've heard it before, and rest assured, I never need to hear it again."

"She ought to have a series of novels written about her—*Mrs. Lillywhite Investigates a Murder in Compartment B2C!*" Frederick blurted proudly.

Serious now, Mr. Tait sat back up in his chair, his

eyes never leaving Rosemary's face, and said, "Do you mean to say Mr. Sutton was murdered? I was under the impression his death was the result of natural causes."

"According to the ship's doctor and the captain, yes," Rosemary agreed, deciding that if the cat was out of the bag, she might as well give it some cream. "However, I disagree. Dolph's lamp had been tampered with, wired to a metal tea tray hidden beneath his desk. He was electrocuted."

Hattie's mouth dropped open in shock for a moment, and then her expression turned to one of avid interest. She leaned forward in her chair. "To think, a real murder on board!" she exclaimed, more excited by the prospect than she ought to have been.

Mr. Tait's eyes, in contrast, narrowed, and his lips pursed beneath his beard. "Are you planning to interrogate us all, then?" he demanded.

"She likely wouldn't *tell* us she was interrogating us, would she, Mr. Tait?" Hattie replied before Rosemary could open her mouth. "In point of fact, she's probably watching our reactions and gathering information right now."

Rosemary thought she heard a trace of a challenge in Hattie's statement, but when her eyes met the young lady's, she found none there and decided she must have imagined it. Even so, Hattie was correct, and Rosemary might have gleaned more information had she not been called out in front of the entire group.

"I'm hardly investigating," she hedged. "The whole sordid ordeal is in the hands of the captain and his security officers who, I'm sure, are more than competent." Rosemary wasn't even remotely convinced of the fact herself, but saying so wouldn't help matters, nor would it do her any good to reveal the bit of information Trix McCoy had shared. If one of them was the killer, it was best to hold some details close to her chest.

Mrs. Long exchanged a worried glance with her husband and began to shake. "Are we in danger? The children—oh!"

"I told you we should have stayed in England," Mr. Long admonished his wife as if it were her fault somehow. Rosemary supposed it was possible Mrs. Long *had* murdered Dolph, but currently, she was at the bottom of the suspect list.

"People rarely kill at random, no matter what the tabloids might have us believe," Rosemary said, trying to sound reassuring. "Most likely, whoever set the trap felt they had good reason to do so. There's no need to panic."

Mrs. Long did not accept that answer. "What if whoever did this decides they, as you say, have good reason to do so *again*?"

"There's at least one of us isn't in any danger at all

because one of us must be the murderer!" Hattie exclaimed, her nostrils flaring when Mrs. Long squeaked in fear.

"Surely not." After gulping twice, Mrs. Long found her voice. "You can't mean to say you think someone from first class would do something so low and so vile as to commit murder. It simply must have been someone from the lower decks. Or at least from another compartment."

Desmond interjected, tossing a disapproving look in Mrs. Long's direction. "I wouldn't be so sure about that. As amenable as the staff may seem, they keep strict tabs on the access between decks."

Mr. Tait glanced between the pair and ultimately came down on Desmond's side. "Not much gets past the stewards," he admitted reluctantly.

"Unless it *was* one of the staff." Leaning back in his chair, Desmond's posture suggested he wasn't taking the matter seriously, but his avid expression disagreed. "The efficient and unobtrusive Stratford, for instance."

Rosemary cocked a brow in his direction, and with a wink, Desmond continued, "I saw him coming out of the Parsons' stateroom looking furtive earlier. He could have been hiding the evidence."

Mr. Tait nodded in agreement with Desmond, accepting the statement. "The question is, who would have wanted him dead?"

Rosemary shrugged sadly. "He never mentioned running into any of his old chums on board, and he was here with his employer, which either leaves us with her as the single suspect or an entire ship full of them."

Calmer now, Mrs. Long agreed. "He did seem a nice man and good with the children."

"Well, I, for one, don't know a thing about anything electrical," Hattie pronounced loudly, "so I certainly couldn't have done it—nor would I have, not to so gentle a soul as Mr. Sutton."

The comment went ignored as Mr. Tait whooshed out an expulsion of air and said to Hattie, "Dear girl, nobody is going to admit to having any knowledge about things electrical now, are they?"

A brief moment of silence ensued until Desmond pointed out helpfully, "Except, Mr. Long has already admitted to being an electrician, has he not?"

Mr. Long's head snapped to attention. He sat up straighter in his chair and leaned over the table. "Now, you wait just a minute; I never said I was an electrician. I work for the electrical service, in an office! I do paperwork. And besides, why would I murder a man I'd never set eyes upon before boarding this ship?"

His voice had become quite loud, and Rosemary thought the way he said the word *ship* made it sound like he could just as easily have meant *a little slice of floating hell*.

Desmond held up his hands in surrender. "Relax, old chap, nobody is accusing you of anything. It was simply an observation. I'm certain you aren't the only soul aboard who could work out how to rewire a lamp. You mark my words, it will turn out to be one of the staff. They've means and opportunity. Given an adequate motive . . ." he trailed off suggestively.

The situation somewhat diffused, Mrs. Long asked the loaded question that Rosemary and her friends had already discussed. "Couldn't the murderer," she shivered at the word, "have set the trap at any time between boarding and when it was tripped? How will they ever find who did it? It seems like the perfect crime."

Rosemary shook her head and said distractedly, "There's no such thing. The killer always makes a mistake."

"Perhaps he already has," Hattie posited, proving her time spent poring over murder mysteries hadn't gone to waste. "We all—with the exception of Mr. Tait, who wasn't there that morning—heard Mr. Sutton say he and Miss McCoy swapped rooms. Could the electrics have been rigged to kill her instead?"

At that, the table exploded with speculation that continued for the rest of the meal. "Our Rosie will get to the bottom of it all," Frederick declared as the group parted ways, causing Mr. Tait to send a disapproving glance in Rosemary's direction.

"Are you quite sure that's wise, dear?" he asked. "You could be putting yourself in harm's way."

"Don't you worry, Mr. Tait," Desmond assured him. "She won't be alone, and she's not the only sleuth amongst us."

CHAPTER TWENTY

Vera finally convinced Rosemary to take a dip in the pool all the way down on F Deck, and the men agreed to tag along. The foursome gathered their swimming clothes and had meandered down the starboard promenade towards the lifts closest to their staterooms when the Verrattis came striding through the doors leading from the opposite side. It was almost like déjà vu, so similar to the afternoon of departure when they were spotted for the first time.

This time, however, Mrs. Verratti recognized Vera and offered a smile. Again, though, Vera was taken aback, for Mrs. Verratti's arm was settled comfortably through her husband's, his hand covering hers like it was a priceless, prized possession.

"Hello," Rosemary said and nodded to the couple. Whatever trouble might be between the couple, Mrs. Verratti looked quite happy at the moment. "

"*Ciao,*" Mrs. Verratti smiled. "Nice day for a

passeggiare, eh?"

"It is," Rosemary agreed, and when Frederick frowned, she explained. "It means to go for a stroll."

"Do you have much Italian?" Mrs. Verratti seemed quite happy to pass a moment or two in idle chat.

"A little," Rosemary said, her smile warm. "It's such a lovely language."

With an irritated glance at her friend, Vera recovered quickly and greeted the singer. "We thought we'd try out the pool. Have you been for a dip yet?"

Mrs. Verratti waved a hand. "Dio no," she said. "It's like a dungeon down there, if you ask me. I prefer to stay as close to the fresh air as possible, isn't that right, darling?"

Her husband smiled and intoned in that velvety voice, "You're a creature of the sun. è vero."

With a vague promise to reschedule the shuffleboard match that had been missed the first day at sea, the Verrattis strolled down the hall towards the most lavish of the first-class staterooms. Rosemary's cheeks pinked at the memory of what she had overheard when she'd found herself down in the Millionaires' Suites the previous evening.

"Rosie, really," Vera huffed after they'd turned the corner and were out of earshot, "you acted like they were ready to claw one another's eyes out! And here they are, looking positively smitten!"

"Perhaps it was just a heated argument," Rosemary suggested. "Or, perhaps they had a late-night reconciliation. It's been known to happen."

In the childish way he and Desmond had when they were children, Frederick coughed to cover a slight, this one aimed at Mr. Verratti. Rosemary distinctly caught the word "dandy" and turned on her brother.

"Not another dig, Frederick. I know you aren't that judgmental—Uncle Herbert was your favorite uncle, and one can hardly call to mind a gentleman *dandier* than him."

All the color drained out of Frederick's face, and his eyes widened. "Uncle Herbert was a pansy?"

Had she been less irritated, it would have been hard for Rosemary not to laugh at the incredulous expression on her naive brother's face. "Father claims he came into the world that way. He also said tolerance, acceptance, and patience were virtues," she added pointedly.

Evidently, the thought that Mr. Verratti might be less interested in his wife than he appeared to be had apparently not occurred to Vera, who wasn't in the least scandalized by a man who, to use Frederick's euphemism, would be considered a *pansy*. She was in show business, after all, where anything widely considered unconventional was more often celebrated than abhorred.

"Poor Mirella," Vera said, now that a possible reason

for the overheard fight had dawned on her. "Such a handsome husband, all for naught. A pity for her. It seems we wives all have our crosses to bear. I'll bet Gianni Verratti doesn't refuse to wear his wife's fashionable gifts."

"If you are referring to that hideous monocle, it's far from fashionable. If I didn't know better, I'd think you were trying to turn me into my father."

Frederick was on his way to ending up with Vera's gift surgically implanted in his nose by way of her fist if he wasn't careful. As it was, his wife marched off and left him to meander toward the lower deck in her wake.

The dip in the pool loosed Rosemary's aching muscles, relaxing her enough to wonder if the pall that had settled over the voyage was merely a figment of her imagination. The foursome exited the lift near compartment B2C, Vera's arm linked through Rosemary's, Frederick and Desmond chatting happily. One could almost forget someone had recently been murdered nearby.

Rosemary attempted to push the thought from her mind, at least long enough to enjoy the moment, but her effort was wasted when a disturbance from the common area caught the group's attention. Their pace quickened, and when Rosemary and her friends rounded the corner, it was to find Mr. and Mrs. Long engaged in a tense, uncomfortable public confrontation.

"What on earth were you thinking, Lois?" Mr. Long shouted at a decibel that set Rosemary's ears ringing. "You've ruined us, don't you know that?"

Mrs. Long cowered on an armchair, her cheeks stained with tears and her eyes red and puffy. "You don't understand, Ric. It isn't my fault!" she cried. Her husband stood over her, his back to Rosemary and her friends, who watched, mesmerized, at the unfolding scene—and they weren't the only ones.

Mr. Long stepped forward menacingly. "You knew what you were doing," he said through clenched teeth. His hands fisted at his sides, and when he began to raise them, Desmond took a step forward. "And you knew this was our only chance to get out of the hole we're in. To get back in the family's good graces!"

Desmond said firmly, "Mr. Long, I think that's enough," a comment Mr. Long duly ignored. Desmond shared a glance with Frederick, who didn't react as far as Rosemary could tell but must have given some sort of secret Boy Scouts signal because Desmond strode purposefully towards the taller man. He tapped Mr. Long on the back, and Mr. Long lost his mind.

He whirled, and Desmond took an elbow to the face, staggering backward into Frederick's arms. Desmond righted himself, touched his lip, and looked at his bloodied hand with an incredulous expression.

With the man being so easily pushed to violence,

Rosemary wondered if Mr. Long had the makings of a master criminal. Could he be the mysterious boss from the conversation she'd overheard? Or worse, could he be Mr. Sutton's killer?

"Whoa, there," Frederick said, stepping in front of Desmond when Mr. Long made another move in his direction.

"My apologies," said Mr. Long, which was the last thing Rosemary had expected to come out of his mouth, though it did appear to have done so at some expense to his pride. "This is not the place to hold a private conversation, and I got carried away. Come now, Lois, let's return to our stateroom."

Mrs. Long began to rise from the armchair, but Desmond took another step forward and said, "Perhaps you ought to calm down first."

When the man turned on Desmond, Rosemary thought fire might pour out of his nose. "This is between myself and my wife. Certainly, you don't presume—"

"Mr. Long," came a voice from the opposite side of the room. Mr. Tait had come through the entrance on the aft side of the common area and now fixed the irate gentleman with a piercing stare. "Mr. Cooper here could turn you in to ship security if you'd rather spend a night in the brig."

"Please, leave my husband alone," Mrs. Long said loud enough for it to be considered a shout and yet somehow still meek. "He's right; I've ruined everything! He didn't intend to strike you, either, Mr. Cooper. He's—"

"Lois, please," her husband implored, the fight having drained out of him now. "Not in front of these strangers."

The lady glanced at Desmond, and then her gaze trailed all the way around the room to land on Rosemary. "We're at our wit's end," she said miserably and sank back down onto the armchair. "I've lost it all. Every penny we had on board, which was nearly every penny we had. We'll be humiliated."

As quickly as she'd pegged Mr. Long for a suspect, Rosemary had to admit he didn't fit the image of either the mysterious boss or Mr. Sutton's killer she'd built in her mind. She might have been wrong, but she couldn't see how a criminal with access to thousands in jewels and American money would be so worried about such a small sum of money. The man looked beaten.

"Oh, Lois," Mr. Long said. He had his eyes closed, his thumb and forefinger pressing into the bridge of his nose. "I don't know what you were thinking. We needed to present ourselves as competent and responsible."

Suddenly, Rosemary felt a little bit sorry for the man—his wife, as well, until the woman added, "I should have won, Ric! But on trick two, Mrs. Parsons led with the King of diamonds!"

183

Vera's eyes narrowed and honed in on Mrs. Long. "She led with a King on trick two?"

"Yes," Mrs. Long replied. "It gave me pause. How did she know he had the Ace of diamond?"

"Something happened during my game," Vera explained. "She made an odd play that I wouldn't expect out of anyone with more than a rudimentary knowledge of bridge, and she acted as though she'd made a mistake but it still worked out in her favor."

When the admission sent everyone into an uproar except for Frederick, his brow furrowed. "What does that mean, precisely? I don't know how to play bridge; I never learned."

Rosemary remembered quite vividly that her brother had remained resolute in his decision to avoid the parlor game. At first, it had been his desire to merely irritate their mother, who was herself quite an enthusiast. Later, he'd simply been stubborn, and now she could tell he wished he'd paid even a smidgen more attention.

"It means," she explained, "that the Parsons are cheating. There's no other explanation." Rosemary regarded Mr. Tait, who was busy steadfastly avoiding her gaze.

Under the weight of her stare, he finally broke. "You're right," he said and motioned for Frederick, who stood closest to the corridor, to ensure they were alone. When he received the all-clear signal, he elucidated.

"I've had my suspicions about the Parsons couple ever since we left Southampton, and poor Mrs. Long has confirmed them. It isn't all that uncommon, really. These ships are a hotbed for all manner of scams and schemes. If it's not cards, it's wagers, and if it's not wagers, it's another form of extortion. Most of the time, the people don't even realize they've been had. Some prey on single men, some on single women, and some on the married ones whose partners are otherwise occupied. If I've read it right, these two are using a divide and conquer strategy."

Frederick sighed then and clapped his hands together. "Mr. Tait is right. It was Mr. Parsons leading the betting—goading people, subtly, into laying down their money or, in some cases, their valuables. I watched one man hand over his watch! And that bit with the cigar, luring Mr. Long into the smoking room so his wife was alone and vulnerable. It's genius—deplorable, but genius."

"It was—it was her, the wife. She pulled me into it, Ric!" Mrs. Long pleaded with her husband, who had still refused to look her square in the eyes, and Rosemary wanted to roll hers skyward. She had watched Mrs. Long the night of the bridge game, and she had hardly been an innocent little lamb being led to slaughter. Clear as day, she recalled the lady's expression, and she was just as positive as she had been then that Mrs. Long was quite willing to engage in a high-stakes game of bridge.

Of course, that didn't mean she'd deserved to get swindled, and Rosemary supposed she probably didn't get out much, considering she had three children to care for. Perhaps she deserved sympathy rather than condemnation after all. Unfortunately, it wasn't Rosemary's to give.

"You have to believe me," Mrs. Long implored her husband, and finally, his eyes met hers.

"I believe Mr. Parsons lured us all to the smoking room that evening. It seems to fit with Mr. Tait's theory," he admitted. "But it doesn't change anything, does it?"

Mrs. Long swallowed back tears and asked, "Can't we tell one of the security officers? Or perhaps lodge a complaint with the Enquiry Office?"

Mr. Tait shook his head. "You could, but it won't do you any good. Unfortunately, you handed your money over of your own volition. I'm afraid there's nothing to be done."

"Like hell, there isn't." Mr. Long jumped up. "I'm getting our money back, one way or another." The desperation showed on his face. "I'll win it back if I have to."

"Not so fast," Desmond interrupted, speaking for the first time since he'd taken Mr. Long's elbow to his lip. "Do you even know how to play bridge?"

"How hard can it be?" Mr. Long asked with a glance

at his wife as if to imply if she could learn how, so could he.

With that, Desmond disagreed. "It's a lot more complicated than it looks, and they're professionals; they'll take your money before you even lay it on the table, and since you don't actually have any money, perhaps you ought to let us help you. I'm a shark, and Vera's no slouch. We'll play for you."

That seemed the last thing Mr. Long had expected, and who could blame him? It wasn't often a man got a fat lip and then offered to help its deliverer out of a bind.

"We have an advantage," Desmond said. "We know what they're doing, how they're doing it. We can swindle the swindlers and maybe even end their little game in the process."

"You're right, Mr. Cooper," said Mr. Tait admiringly. The older gentleman's eyes twinkled. "You'll need my help as well, but first, we'll need to watch them; work out their signals so we can turn the tables."

Mr. Long, though grateful, was also impatient. "And what precisely am I supposed to do until then? Just sit around knowing we've been bankrupted and our time is running out?"

The question came out as a shout, and in the moment of silence that followed, the entire room was surprised to hear the sound of a choked sob coming from the threshold between the common room and the Longs' wing of the compartment.

It was little Rose, who was now being swaddled into her older brother's arms. Young Stewart's eyes never left his father's face as he backed away, until finally he turned, and Mr. Long's shoulders sagged, the fight draining out of him.

Gently, Frederick broke his relative silence and admonished the man. "What you're going to do is pull it together. For your children, who don't deserve any of this and also ought never to know anything about it."

It was an unusual position for Frederick to take, but Rosemary realized that perhaps she'd not given her brother enough credit in the past. Even during his wanton days as an eligible bachelor, he'd always come through for her in a critical moment—perhaps not as frequently as she'd been required to return the favor, but often enough to count.

CHAPTER TWENTY-ONE

It occurred to Rosemary to protest Desmond and Frederick's valiant plot to foil the Parsons couple's bridge scheme. To her mind, investigating Dolph's murder was of higher priority, yet, injustice in any form galled. The Longs weren't the first victims to fall for the Parsons couple's deception, nor would they be the last. Not unless someone stepped in to stop them.

The clincher had been Frederick's statement regarding the Long children, which had tugged at Rosemary's heartstrings. It called to mind the soft curve of innocent Rose's little pink cheek and the pain in the boy's eyes. None of them had asked for their mother to behave irresponsibly, but they would suffer sorely for it if the damage wasn't reversed and the money recovered.

When she and her friends returned to the privacy of Frederick and Vera's suite, Rosemary said, "I didn't want to discuss it in front of the others, but ever since you mentioned Mr. Parsons accepting a watch as payment, I've been thinking—what if the suitcase with the diamonds and cash belongs to them? What if this scheme of theirs is bigger than we realize, and Mr. Parsons is the fearsome boss I heard those two thugs talking about?"

Frederick's head tilted to one side. "It's possible, and if so, problem solved. We've already got the Longs' money and then some. I can't believe you checked the suitcase in to the purser without showing me and Des, Rosie. You're a terrible sister and a worse traveling companion."

As she frequently did, Rosemary ignored her brother's dig. "Even if the loot does belong to the Parsons, us stealing it isn't justice." Ever since Mr. Tait mentioned the ship's brig, she had been picturing the duplicitous couple locked inside its cage and found she rather fancied the notion.

"No, but the loot could be the leverage we need to bring them down," Desmond said thoughtfully, "*if*, of course, it belongs to them in the first place."

Rosemary agreed. "We need confirmation, and we need to tread lightly. I say we find out as much as we can about the pair—you men tail Mr. Parsons; Vera and I will follow his wife."

With that, it was decided, and for the rest of the afternoon, Rosemary and Vera tried to look innocent while stalking Mrs. Parsons all over the ship. After a lunch of cod fillets and rice pudding, the object of their interest visited the cigarette stand and then strolled the promenade for a long while, smoking and staring out to sea. Then it was up to the Boat Deck for a drink at the Observation Lounge bar.

"She's done nothing of reproach except perhaps purchase that god-awful green brocade suit," Vera whined after they'd followed the woman, at a safe distance, around the shops for an hour. "I'm bored."

They had come to a stop on C Deck, where Mrs. Parsons picked up a telegram from the correspondence station, so close to where Rosemary's adventure had begun the previous evening, just a short way aft near the second-class entrance.

When their quarry ducked into the beauty salon, it was more than Vera could take. "Let's go in and indulge ourselves, Rosie. They serve champagne while you wait—it'll take the edge off, and then we can continue to totter along behind this horrible woman for as long as you like."

It wouldn't do to let Vera know she'd been having a similar thought—although Rosemary would have preferred to swap the champagne and nails with another perusal of the B Deck library—it became a moot point when Mrs. Verratti ducked into the salon behind Mrs. Parsons.

Vera's fingers tightened around her forearm, and

Rosemary resigned herself to her fate.

"Come on." Rosemary let Vera grovel anyway. "We're traveling first class, after all. It isn't as though we'd appear out of place enjoying a bit of pampering. And besides, how many secrets have we been privy to while waiting for our nails to dry? We might learn more following her inside than we have all afternoon."

"All right," Rosemary surrendered. "We aren't getting anywhere doing it my way, that's for sure."

"You're an absolute saint, Rosie," Vera replied with a satisfied smile. With a wink, she went to work cajoling the receptionist into revealing what treatments her previous two customers had selected and practically purred when it turned out they were both having their hairstyles refreshed in the salon. "Perhaps your luck is turning—or maybe it's just mine rubbing off on you."

"Either way, I'll take it," Rosemary replied.

The salon wasn't a cavernous room by any means. Hairstyling stations spaced at intervals lined all three walls, and in the center sat two banks of dryer stations, back-to-back.

Much to Vera's disappointment, the seats on either side of Mrs. Verratti's prime location in the center of the room were already taken. Rosemary heard the singer ask the young lady sitting to her right if she had a boyfriend and was surprised when Mrs. Verratti sounded authentically interested in the answer.

Mrs. Parsons, in contrast, perched on one of the chairs along the opposite wall, jiggling her leg impatiently. She barely noticed when Rosemary and Vera entered, so intent was she on berating the hairdresser. "I just need a flash of air and a spritz of spray. Quickly now, I've things to do, and I mustn't be late!"

Immediately, Rosemary regretted having been sympathetic to Vera's plea, for their quarry would soon be lost—just as Vera was now lost to her idol. They were shown to stations facing away from Mrs. Verratti, their backs to both the singer and Mrs. Parsons. However, with so many mirrors, Rosemary could observe both of the ladies without either of them noticing, and so she settled in to see if, perhaps, she'd been hasty in judging the excursion a failure.

Impatient, Mrs. Parsons made no attempt at chitchat, choosing instead to maintain her sour expression, but Mrs. Verratti looked entirely at ease and, in fact, quite entertained by the young ladies who gazed at her adoringly.

"He's lovely, really. I shouldn't complain," said the girl sitting next to Mrs. Verratti. Rosemary caught snippets of the conversation in between the sound of the hair dryers going on and off. "I simply can't decide if he's the one."

Mirella Verratti waved her hand and said with sincerity, "Darling girl, when true love strikes, you know it in your bones—he's the one! But if there's one piece of advice I could give you, it would be this: true love is hard to come by. It's the exception, not the rule. You could wait around forever—it's a risk. Choose wisely."

The indecisive girl's face turned pensive while her friend sighed, "I'd kill to have a husband like yours," and Mrs. Verratti's face lit with a fond smile. Rosemary watched her, wondering what the truth of their relationship really was.

Furthermore, she wondered if what the lady said was true. She herself had already had one true love in her young life: Andrew Lillywhite, hands down. And yet, there was Max, and he was certainly worth swooning over. She would be lucky to spend her life with him, but was it asking too much for him to follow in her late husband's footsteps? The more concerning question of whether she was truly uncertain or simply running scared threatened to surface, but she tamped it down and forced her mind to return to the investigation.

When Rosemary and Vera exited the salon twenty minutes later, every hair on their heads had been expertly styled and lacquered into place, but Mrs. Parsons was nowhere to be found.

"Drat, Where might she have gone?" Rosemary asked, scanning the corridor for any trace of the woman and finding none. She did see Hattie sitting in an armchair near the bottom of the stairs, her face in a book. Rosemary wondered if she was rereading Miss McCoy's novel and shook her head at the idea that someone could be so obviously and unabashedly sycophantic.

Vera rolled her eyes and said sourly, "There isn't a nook or cranny on this ship we haven't followed that woman through today, and we haven't learned a thing of importance. I couldn't begin to imagine where she's off to now."

Mrs. Parsons *had* led them on what felt like a wild goose chase. "Do you think she knows?" Rosemary asked. "I mean that we were following her."

With a frown, Vera said, "I should certainly hope not. We were discreet, don't you think?"

As discreet as someone like Vera could ever expect to be, Rosemary supposed. Her friend wasn't the type to blend into a crowd.

Rosemary went to stand near the lift, but Vera grabbed her arm and pulled her towards the stairs. "Let's walk for the sake of my thighs," she implored.

"*My* thighs are still burning from my last experience with the stairs," Rosemary complained but received no sympathy.

Instead, Vera pouted and continued to press. "I still can't believe you went gallivanting about the ship without me."

"If it didn't take you three hours to dress for dinner,"

Rosemary shot back, "perhaps I wouldn't have had to."

Vera wasn't the least bit chagrined and forged on, taking the steps at a higher speed than Rosemary could handle. She tried to keep pace until she noticed Trix McCoy on the landing up ahead and stopped short. Only then did she remember the author's abhorrence of the lift.

"Wait," Rosemary hissed, "I would prefer not to encounter that woman again today if at all possible. Also, you're going too fast. What part of *I climbed a million flights of stairs yesterday* do you not understand, Vera?"

"Aaahh!" Miss McCoy let out a scream that rang through the stairwell. At the same time, something heavy-sounding banged off the railing and what felt like a spray of buckshot came whizzing past Rosemary's head.

Impulsively, Vera dove on top of her friend, shielding Rosemary's body with her own, just as whatever had fallen made contact with the stairs on the next landing down.

From below, where she had been sitting and reading her book, Hattie came running. Her eyes widened as she took in the scene before her—Trix McCoy sprawled on the landing above, Rosemary and Vera in a heap on the one below, pea-sized ball bearings all over the floor. She helped Vera up, and they both got Rosemary to her feet, then carefully climbed the stairs to set a moaning Miss McCoy back to rights.

Ignoring her own safety in favor of curiosity, Vera stepped to the railing and leaned over to look upward for the source of what had very nearly constituted the author's doom.

"Vera, be careful," Rosemary admonished before turning to Trix McCoy. "Are you quite all right?"

Eyes glazed, the author didn't immediately answer, but she also didn't appear to be badly injured aside from a few bumps and red marks that would surely turn to bruises over the next few hours.

Miss McCoy stared at the cloth bag that Vera had picked up off the floor. Its drawstring had broken open on the way down in a fortuitous accident. Had the bag remained intact, the combined weight of the ball bearings in it could have knocked her out—even killed her, perhaps. In breaking open and showering the stairwell with their spray, Miss McCoy's life might have been spared.

Rosemary watched as the realization dawned on Miss McCoy, and saw the fear in her eyes before Molly arrived and offered to escort the author back to her stateroom.

"Perhaps we ought to take the lift just this once, madam," the stewardess implored, and this time there was no fight left in Miss McCoy as she leaned on

Molly's arm.

After the two women had gone and someone from the stewards' bureau had been commissioned to clean up the mess, Hattie approached Rosemary, her brow furrowed thoughtfully. "Are you really investigating Mr. Sutton's murder?" she asked, taking Rosemary aback with her frankness.

"I don't have my spyglass with me at the moment," she replied dryly, "but I suppose, in a manner of speaking, yes."

Hattie lowered her voice. "I'm worried about Miss McCoy," she said. The admission didn't come as much of a shock given what had just occurred, but the young lady seemed to think it ought to. She followed behind Rosemary and Vera as they continued up the stairs and into the B2C compartment, chattering all the way about means, motive, and opportunity until again Rosemary had to press her, forcefully, off.

"I'm quite spent, Hattie, really. It's been quite a long day, and of course, I need to get dressed for dinner," she said pointedly.

Her cheeks turning a delicate shade of pink, Hattie apologized and tottered off down the hall. Rosemary could have sworn she was talking nineteen to the dozen as she went, even though there wasn't anyone around to hear her!

Chapter Twenty-Two

Dinner that evening was a drab affair; by night four, the passengers had begun to feel restless, anticipating the end of the voyage and their arrival in New York. Those who had boarded aspiring to secure a love match were becoming more desperate by the day, as evidenced by the rising hemlines and shrinking necklines all across the Grand Saloon.

And, of course, at Rosemary's table, the hovering pall of Dolph Sutton's death—and Miss McCoy's subsequent accident—did nothing to improve the atmosphere. The author, of course, had declined to attend dinner, and Rosemary wondered if she would stay in her stateroom clear through the final night and miss the Verrattis' highly anticipated performance altogether.

Anxious to set the plan for regaining their money in motion, the Longs glared daggers at the Parsons who, seated at their usual table on the other side of the staircase, remained oblivious to the animosity simply pouring off the couple.

Indeed, they were nearly as oblivious as Hattie, the only one with no knowledge of the scheme planned for that evening. Everyone involved knew their responsibilities, but when Hattie excused herself to the powder room, Rosemary ran through the details one last time.

"Freddie insists he's rubbish at bridge and insists he never gets to do anything fun," Rosemary tossed a rueful glance at her brother, "so he and I will borrow the key to the cargo hold and check the Parsons' luggage for their winnings." It had sounded like a plausible enough reason to convince the Longs and Mr. Tait.

Only Rosemary and her traveling companions knew the full reason for the cargo hold excursion, and she intended to keep it that way. To her mind, they could kill two, maybe even three birds with one stone if it turned out the Parsons couple was also responsible for the mysterious case full of jewels as well as Dolph's death. It was a long shot, but there were too many unanswered questions for Rosemary's taste.

"Meanwhile," she continued, "Desmond and Vera, as our best bridge players, will match the Parsons play-for-play and win back the Longs' money. It ought not to be terribly difficult now that we know their ploy. Mrs. Long, Mr. Long, and Mr. Tait will retire to the common area and stake out the Parsons' suite. If anything goes awry, one of you will come for me and Fred, and one will fetch Vera and Des. Is everyone clear?"

Only Desmond's voice was missing from the chorus of agreement, and when Rosemary glanced in his direction, she noticed him gazing over at one of the tables full of preening women. The one who'd had her eyes on him since the first day aboard batted her eyelashes seductively. Rosemary could see why he'd become distracted; the sight was a veritable buffet for the eyes, but she pulled him back to reality with a well-aimed kick to his shin beneath the tablecloth that, for once, he didn't have time to deflect.

"Ouch!" he cried, his head whipping back to attention. "I've got it, Rose," he said irritably.

A tart retort on the tip of her tongue, Rosemary didn't have a chance to deliver it because the band's song finished, and before the brief pause before the start of the next one had ended, the sound of angry voices pierced the air.

"I don't have time for this. Look at all these people waiting for me to sing." Mrs. Verratti stood, facing her husband as if he were a bull and she the matador tasked with taking him down. Her chest heaved with emotion, and her eyes sparkled.

Even though the band continued playing, the volume level across the rest of the saloon plummeted towards silence.

"How much higher a pedestal could you possibly require?" Mr. Verratti fired back. "The entire world adores you."

Rosemary felt a wave of déjà vu. She was certain that not only had she heard this argument before, she knew exactly what was coming next.

Sure enough, Mrs. Verratti defended herself and her career, and then Mr. Verratti took a deep breath and spoke the words that had felt unduly harsh the first time Rosemary heard them.

"You belong to your fans, Mirella, to the masses and the press. Not to me—never to me! I cannot compete with them, and I don't wish to try anymore."

"The public does not control me. Nor do you." Mirella tossed her head, then lifted her chin. "Jealousy is a most unattractive trait in a man."

Absently mouthing along, Rosemary caught the look on Vera's face and tensed her jaw to stop herself. Husbands and wives might have the same argument more than once—goodness knows she'd heard her mother berate her father for continuing habits she found deplorable. Even within her own marriage to Andrew had been the occasional dispute but never, not once in her recollection, had a disagreement been repeated verbatim.

Having spent enough time watching Vera rehearse for a role, Rosemary's instincts fairly screamed that this couple had staged that argument—practiced to get it just right. It fit with the rumor the stewardess from the Millionaire's Suites had perpetrated the first day at sea. The question was why, and it was one with many possible answers.

Mr. Verratti raised his voice. "Call me ugly if you must, but do not ask me to play second fiddle in your orchestra. It's over!"

A graceful hand waved in dismissal. "Very well." Mirella Verratti's chin lifted in defiance. "If an end is what you want, then an end is what you shall get." Dark eyes flashing, the singer tossed her head and stalked from the room.

All expression wiped from his face, her husband repeated the performance in the opposite direction. He'd no more than disappeared from sight when the stunned silence turned to an uproar.

Vera would want to dissect this moment the first chance she got Rosemary alone, but that would have to wait. For now, there was work to be done.

Chapter Twenty-Three

Divesting the chap manning the stewards' counter of the key to the cargo hold wasn't terribly difficult. All Rosemary had to do was bat her eyelashes in a fair impression of the young lady who had captured Desmond's attention at dinner while Frederick nonchalantly nipped it from its hook.

First, however, they had checked into the purser's safety deposit box for the treasure-filled suitcase, partly to make sure it was still there and intact, but mostly because Frederick was dying for a proper look at the contents.

"I really ought not to go into this mission blind, don't you think?" he had cajoled. Now he said, "You really do have the strangest luck, Rosie," his eyes bright with the reflection of a fortune in diamonds. "I know I've certainly never been erroneously delivered a case full of jewels."

"You've also never stumbled upon a dead body,"

Rosemary retorted. "Are you certain you want to covet my luck?"

She led her brother to the lifts and took a more direct route to the first-class cargo hold, keen to avoid the second-class section where she didn't dare trespass again. Every ounce of the so-called "luck" Freddie thought she possessed was sorely needed elsewhere!

"Through here," she said, quickly unlocking the door and slipping quietly through and into the hold. Once inside, Frederick did a sweep to make sure he and Rosemary were alone and then wedged the door closed with a broom handle for good measure.

The pair found themselves in a cavernous, humid storage space with endless cell-like cages. At various intervals, rope nets filled with cargo hung from overhead. The sheer volume of goods—carefully wrapped pieces of priceless antique furniture and towering stacks of color-coordinated trunks and cases—created a labyrinthine effect and caused Rosemary's spirits to plummet to the floor.

"It's hopeless. We'll never find what we're looking for among all this," she lamented, wiping away the sweat that had already begun to accumulate above her brow. "Not before we melt."

Frederick scoffed. "Not with that attitude, we won't. Look, there's a system." He pointed to labels tacked to each cage. "We only need to find our compartment."

Indeed, it didn't take long to realize they were laid out in the same pattern as the staterooms a few decks above, compartment B2C clearly marked. Inside, every stateroom's luggage had been divided into piles, each covered with rope netting to keep the contents from sliding all over the place and marked with the ticket holder's name.

Frederick made to enter, but Rosemary hesitated. "Are we really doing this? Snooping through our traveling neighbors' personal property?"

Her brother came back and slung an arm around her shoulders. "Rosie, there are bad people in our compartment. People who have fleeced many other passengers—some more, but some much less fortunate. Those people deserve to be brought down."

"Of course they do, but do two wrongs suddenly make a right? Are we the law now?" she asked.

"You sound like Max," Frederick replied. "Or our mother, and for the record, even Evelyn Woolridge would agree the Parsons need to learn their lesson. She certainly wouldn't abide murder. If Mr. Parsons is the big bad boss, he could have killed Dolph. That's why we're here, not to snoop. We've a moral obligation to at least try to bring this boss—whoever he is—down," he cajoled.

Rosemary shivered, and her resolve cracked. "Jimmy and Tony were not nice men—if they'd found me eavesdropping, there's no telling what they might have done—and *they* were scared of the boss," she said. "Whoever he is, he's unscrupulous, and at this point, the only person who fits that description is Mr. Parsons."

Frederick winked and said, "See, little sister, it's a good thing you brought me with you. Who else could convince you to give up your morals as easily as me?"

"It's your special talent, Freddie," she replied as she entered the caged area containing the B2C compartment passengers' luggage. He tried to slip in behind her, but there simply wasn't room.

"Perhaps if my wife hadn't packed our entire house to take to America, I could fit in there with you, but as it stands, this whole compartment is packed to the gills. Why don't I just have a look around?" Frederick suggested, and Rosemary could practically see him vibrating with excitement over the prospect of exploring the rest of the hold.

"Go on, Freddie," Rosemary said distractedly, recognizing her own luggage in a pile in the corner. While her brother wandered off in the other direction, Rosemary pulled aside the netting covering her trunks. After a thorough inspection, she concluded that everything, except the suitcase that had been missing all along, was present and accounted for.

Then, she noticed a piece of emerald-green fabric tucked in between two trunks and felt the blood rise to her cheeks. Rosemary tugged on the edge of the closest trunk, revealing a pile of crumpled crepe de Chine.

She let out a mild but loud expletive and received a distracted "You all right?" from somewhere within the depths of the hold.

"My dresses!" she exclaimed. She'd felt no particular attachment to them when Vera had insisted on their purchase but seeing them crumpled like that felt like a waste, both of money and fine French craftsmanship.

She gathered them up, along with the undergarments that had also been carelessly discarded, and stowed them in one of her other trunks. If she was caught trespassing in the cargo hold while carrying an armload of brassieres and knickers, she might actually die—of embarrassment.

Rosemary stood up and looked around their compartment's section of the hold with renewed interest. She had been under the impression that one of the stewards had simply mistaken the case with the jewels for her own, but why then would hers have been emptied, and where was it now?

Her earlier hesitation having flown, Rosemary began a thorough search of the hold. Vera and Frederick's taupe luggage was piled neatly next to Desmond's two paltry trunks. Trix McCoy's case striped with canary yellow and burnt orange sadly were stacked next to Dolph's cases, all of which appeared untouched since having been deposited there in Southampton.

Next, her eyes raked over Mr. Tait's royal-blue baggage striped patriotically with red and white— nothing out of the ordinary there. The trunks and cases were all in excellent shape, covered in the stamps and labels of a seasoned traveler, and again, none appeared to have been touched since boarding.

Rosemary's suitcase seemed to have been the only one vandalized, and she had a sinking feeling the whole excursion had been for naught. Her dismay lasted until she pulled the netting off the last remaining stack of luggage to reveal a set of familiar-looking cream-colored cases.

They were quite similar to her own and an exact match for the one with the diamonds and cash—there was no other possibility. Rosemary's heart leaped to her throat and then plummeted all the way down to the pit of her stomach. Before she could confirm the validity of the sinking feeling, Frederick bellowed from the other side of the hold.

"Uh, Rosie, come here." She didn't notice the urgency in his voice, not even when he called again, more loudly this time. "Rosemary!"

"What, Freddie?" she called back. "I'm in the middle of something here."

"For God's sake, Rose, could you just come here?" her brother shouted, rousing her from her dazed state. She tore her eyes away from Hattie's luggage and forced herself to focus on her brother, weaving her way through the stacks of trunks towards his voice.

"What is it?" she asked, finally finding him standing behind the first of a row of coffins, the lid open and his face ashen. She let out a shiver and took a step back before she could see what was inside. "What on earth are you doing? Is there a body in there? Is it Dolph?"

Frederick took a step out from behind the coffin, his face a mask of disgust. "Of course not. Do you think they'd keep a body down here? In this heat? Just come here," he said, waving her over.

Rosemary swallowed hard and steeled herself, resisting the urge to shield her eyes from whatever was inside. She needn't have worried because Frederick hadn't been lying. There wasn't a dead body inside—in fact, there was nothing inside at all. Annoyed, she said, "Why would you scare me like that?"

"Look closer," her brother insisted, "at the lining." Upon further inspection, Rosemary realized the coffin's lining did look a bit thicker than it ought to have. Only a very small or thin person would fit inside, she noticed, deciding she would need at least three gin and tonics to get that thought out of her head.

The irony of the thought occurred to her almost immediately when Frederick handed her a bottle filled with amber liquid.

"I've seen this before," Rosemary said, a feeling of

dread settling into the pit of her stomach, "and so have you."

"I know, Rosie," he replied. "It was only twenty minutes ago. This is the same rum as was in the suitcase with the diamonds. The two are connected."

Her brain went into puzzle-solving mode. "Jimmy and Tony mentioned coffins. At the time, I thought they were making a joke, but this is what they meant. Also, Trix McCoy was right. There *is* a band of rum-smugglers aboard this ship! Do you think she knew about it? Do you think that's why Dolph is dead?" The question was rhetorical because Rosemary didn't give her brother a chance to reply.

Over the years, Frederick Woolridge had learned that when his sister—or any member of the fairer sex, for that matter—began babbling, it was best to just let her continue until she ran out of steam. Interrupting, offering advice, and certainly, raising any sort of counterpoint would not be considered wise, and though Frederick usually took an immature pride in his lack of wisdom, when it came to women, he'd concluded that knowledge was most definitely power.

"Maybe Dolph found out about the rum. He did say he needed to fetch his spare inhaler from the cargo hold. He might have happened upon the coffin himself and painted a target on his back."

Frederick remained silent, waiting for whatever was

happening inside his sister's head to pop out of her mouth and becoming quite concerned that perhaps they might have been better off leaving well enough alone. She would come to a conclusion—most likely the right one—when she'd run through all the possibilities. In Frederick's opinion, the man who had labeled women as dim was a very stupid man indeed.

"No, that can't be; Miss McCoy told Hattie about the plot of her next book *before* Dolph mentioned visiting the cargo hold. Miss McCoy told Hattie," Rosemary repeated, what she'd seen in the B2C compartment's section of the hold finally sinking in. "Hattie! The suitcase with the diamonds matches the luggage listed as belonging to her stateroom. She's either mixed up in this and likely in quite over her head, or whoever tampered with my luggage also tampered with hers. I can't imagine why, however."

Now, Rosemary appeared puzzled. "Did Hattie know about the rum smuggling when Trix McCoy revealed her upcoming book's subplot? The pin from the case looked quite similar to those worn by the stewards. Do you think Stratford is involved?"

Frederick rubbed his chin as he gave the matter some thought. "Stratford as the mysterious boss makes more sense than either old Mr. Tait or Mr. Parsons. He's worked on this line for a while, knows all the ins and outs."

"All three of them do, though, don't they? Mr. Tait is a frequent traveler, and the Parsons didn't start this con of theirs yesterday. Perhaps they hop from ship to ship and only visit a particular one infrequently enough not to be noticed, but they're definitely seasoned voyagers."

Reluctantly, Frederick admitted, "I suppose so, but where does that leave us, then?"

Shrugging, Rosemary said, "What I can't get my head around is: what does any of this have to do with Dolph's death?"

"I don't know, but we need to get out of here, Rosie," Frederick implored. "Work out what this means in the safety of our staterooms. I don't think either of us wants to be found having discovered what's in this coffin. It's hundreds of pounds worth of illegal spirits. It really *is* enough to kill over."

Rosemary wondered aloud, "Why do you and Vera know the market prices of so many stolen goods?"

"You're going to have to explain that comment to me later," her brother replied, a quizzical expression flitting across his face before he hustled her out of there and back to the relative safety of the first-class entrance.

Chapter Twenty-Four

During the trek back to B Deck, Rosemary maintained hope that the other component of the mission—finding a way to foil the Parsons couple—had gone according to plan. However, her heart sank when she and Frederick arrived in the compartment common room, sticky from their humid trip to the cargo hold. Desmond's hanging head said it all, but Mr. Long's long face left no room for doubt.

Over at the drinks trolley, Mr. Tait waved a decanter of brandy over a tray of glasses without much concern for how much made it into each one and then downed a shot in one gulp.

"What's happened?" Rosemary and Frederick asked simultaneously, accepting one of the slippery glasses handed around by Mr. Tait.

Off to one side, Desmond leaned forward in his seat on the padded armchair and rested his elbows on his knees. "It's my fault. I got distracted," he explained, holding aloft the hand that wasn't clutching a glass of amber courage. His knuckles were wrapped in a white bandage, and when he turned to fully face Frederick and Rosemary, she noticed a cut near the corner of his right eye.

"On my way to the lounge, I happened upon one of those young ladies from the table across from ours at dinner," Desmond explained reluctantly, knowing his friends wouldn't allow the conversation to move forward until they knew what had transpired.

"Don't tell me you were *distracted* the same way you were at dinner," Rosemary warned, remembering the expression he'd worn earlier.

Frederick guffawed, earning himself a glare from Mr. Long.

Desmond grimaced and shook his head, then frowned again. "She was being maltreated by some cad near the men's toilet. What was I to do? Let her suffer?"

Somehow, Desmond did always manage to come up smelling of roses. Leave it to him to have become waylaid by carrying out a noble act, slipping out of everyone's bad graces just like he and Frederick always had since they were children.

Vera, who had moved over on the settee to make room for her husband, took up the explanation. "I couldn't get into a game; they were only hosting men's' teams, and without Desmond . . ."

Her eyes shifted towards the drinks trolley where Mr. Tait stood next to Mr. Long. The latter had yet to speak, and Mrs. Long looked as though she might soon burst into tears, but since she'd been the one to get her husband into the mess in the first place, she wisely kept quiet.

"We didn't fare so well," Mr. Tait said grimly just as Mr. Long announced, "It's my fault. I missed the cues because I can't hear out of my right ear."

Rosemary remembered how surprised he'd been earlier that afternoon when he'd elbowed Desmond in the face and now understood why, often, he'd appeared detached from his family's conversations. It must have been difficult for him, especially since he seemed like a man who loathed admitting weakness.

"Sometimes, especially on this ship," Mr. Long explained, "all I can hear is a monotonous hum. Damn it!" He hurled his glass towards the wood paneling and seemed almost disappointed when it didn't shatter into a million pieces and instead bounced off and rolled beneath an end table on the other side of the room.

Mrs. Long now appeared embarrassed as well as distraught, and Rosemary wondered if she was going to make it to New York without a complete mental breakdown.

"Whoa now," Frederick said, descending upon Mr. Long. "There's no need for that. We still have time to work out another way."

Mr. Long's eyes flashed, and his jaw tightened. "It must be wonderful not to worry about money, to be able to spend all your time in leisure, reading comics and acting like a child, but we can't all—"

"And that's the rub, isn't it?" Frederick interrupted. "This isn't just about the cards. It's about your son, who can't stand being in the same room as you."

Now it wasn't just his eyes flashing that made Mr. Long appear feral. "How dare you talk about my son!" he exclaimed, ready to pounce.

Had his words been directed towards Desmond, the evening might have ended differently; he'd already been in one physical altercation and was still quite ramped up. Frederick, however, had recently learned a valuable lesson about his temper. A year before, he'd been suspected of murder after an evening of too much gin, and Rosemary had been forced to prove his innocence. Since then, her brother had grown into a man who, though he still enjoyed fun and games, no longer felt inclined to rise to the occasion when it came to physical violence.

"It's not me you're angry with, Mr. Long," Frederick said diplomatically, taking a step back, "it's yourself, but it's not too late to improve your relationship with your son. You can try finding something in common with him or take it out on me, but I'm not going to fight you. I'm going to help you, for Stewart's sake—but you need to calm down and stop trying to go toe to toe with me, do you understand?"

Judging by the look in Vera's eye, Frederick's speech had done more than just impassion Mr. Long. Still, she thought it best to intervene.

"Gentlemen, if we could get back to the business at hand." Assessing Mr. Long for a moment, Rosemary remembered something she'd read about people who were hard of hearing. "It doesn't matter what you heard, Mr. Long. I'm far more interested in what you saw. They're communicating somehow, the Parsons, by some sort of code. Close your eyes for a moment and think. Did you happen to notice anything unusual during the game? Maybe something Mr. Parsons did more than once?"

Looking skeptical, Mr. Long did as he was told, closed his eyes, and played back the memory of what he'd seen. After another long moment, his mouth rounded.

"He fidgeted with his cigarette case."

Frowning, Rosemary asked, "Fidgeted how?"

Mr. Long explained, "He moved it around on the table almost absentmindedly. He even shook it on occasion, but only during bidding—during *every* bid, come to think. I didn't really pay that much attention at the time because it seemed like one of those things people do,"

He pointed toward Desmond. "For instance, you tap your fingers on your leg when you see a pretty woman."

As Desmond had been looking at Rosemary and doing that exact thing, he hastily shoved the offending hand into his pocket and ignored the blush that stole over her face.

"I do not," he said in self-defense, but with no heat to the words, as everyone could see they weren't true.

"This is good." She asked a few more questions, and a smile that wasn't entirely ladylike but almost feral lit Rosemary's face. "This is very good indeed."

"Rosie to the rescue." Frederick stood and, going to his sister, lifted her off her feet and gave her a smacking kiss on the lips. "You're something; did you know that?"

Agreement with that assessment came from all corners of the room. Within a few minutes, the group had a plan in motion. The Parsons wouldn't know what had hit them.

CHAPTER TWENTY-FIVE

All through the night, visions of Hattie Humphries' suitcase full of diamonds chased away sleep. Tossing and turning, Rosemary considered possible connections between it and Dolph's death, between Miss McCoy and Dolph's death, and where the Parsons' wagering scheme fit into the picture.

No matter how she tried to fit the pieces together, the puzzle wouldn't come clear. Too many missing bits to get the full picture. Or maybe the problem was there were too many pieces altogether.

On balance, Rosemary knew she should at least attempt to alert Captain Hughes to the hotbed of illicit activity going on both above and below decks on his ship. And if he hadn't already proved what little regard he held for her investigative prowess, Rosemary might have done just that.

Briefly, she considered approaching Hattie directly and asking point-blank whether the suitcase and the rum were related to the murder. In light of Jimmy and Tony's instincts about the head of the operation's temperament, she decided the girl probably wouldn't dare to give her a straight answer.

It was close to dawn when one thought gave way to another and caused Rosemary to sit straight up in bed. What if Dolph's death *wasn't* connected to the smuggled rum, the Parsons, or the mysterious boss at all? What if it only looked that way because it had all happened at once and in close proximity?

What if the trap had been set to target the author all along? Or, even more concerning, Rosemary herself? Someone had dropped a bag of ball bearings down a stairwell with no care for whoever might have been making use of the stairs at that moment, and she was no closer to working out who had done it than she was to the truth about anything else.

Or, what if Trix McCoy herself—the one person close enough to Dolph to actually have a valid motive for wanting him dead—killed him and set the trap in the stairwell as a diversion? That theory didn't fit with Rosemary's perception of Trix, but experience had taught her that people were often capable of far more than they let on.

The only thing she *was* certain of was that the ship's arrival in New York loomed. They would dock within a day's time, and if something wasn't done, not only would a murderer walk free, but so would a pair of swindlers and a group of rumrunners!

Perhaps Rosemary could solve at least one of those mysteries, and to do so, she needed to talk to Trix McCoy. One way or another, the author knew more than she had let on, and Rosemary wanted answers. The only one she refused to accept was *no*.

Time passed slowly while she waited for a reasonable hour to go calling, then Rosemary held her breath as she knocked on the stateroom door, fully prepared to once again be rebuffed. Instead, when she asked the author, "May I speak to you? It's important," Miss McCoy sighed and bade her entrance.

"What can I do for you, Mrs. Lillywhite?" she asked warily but took a seat in one of the armchairs and indicated Rosemary should take the other. "I expected it would only be a matter of time before you came back, pressing."

"I know you're withholding information—important information that might help bring a murderer to justice," Rosemary answered, not bothering to beat around the bush. "Believe it or not, I can keep a secret. Whatever it is you're hiding will be safe with me. Unless what you're hiding is that you killed Dolph. I won't be a party to murder, even after the fact."

Several moments passed while the author contemplated what, if anything, to say. Waiting patiently, Rosemary resisted the urge to push. Poking a mule in the backside was just as likely to make it balk as to get it moving. While comparing Miss McCoy to a pack animal wasn't the most charitable thing to do, Rosemary couldn't help thinking that pound for pound, the resemblance was there.

Finally, with a great sigh, Miss McCoy gave in. "I did not kill my secretary. His death, in fact, has put me in a most difficult position. Ask your questions, and I will answer them truthfully."

The first one that sprang to Rosemary's mind was the one Miss McCoy had just answered, but the author was still hiding something. Was it murder, or was it something else—perhaps of a personal nature?

"Can you describe your relationship with Mr. Sutton? Did it go beyond working together?"

The answer came quickly and with a snort that landed somewhere between derision and amusement. "I've any number of better things to do with my time than chase around after the male of the species."

Or the female, Rosemary inferred from the tone and timbre of Miss McCoy's denial. A true spinster.

"Nevertheless, it would be disingenuous for me to imply that he was nothing more than a secretary as Mr. Sutton was invaluable to my work." Such ineffable sadness washed over the author's face that Rosemary couldn't help softening.

"We are both intelligent, capable women who ought to be on the same side. I liked Dolph, Trix, and I know you genuinely cared for him. Help me find the person responsible because I'm not certain, even now, that he was the intended victim or if one of us was meant to end up dead."

Trix McCoy kept her nose firmly lifted in the air for a long moment. Rosemary's stomach fluttered. She recognized the feeling—the little thrill of adrenaline when a suspect or a witness cracked under the pressure of a thorough interrogation—or, in this case, a few sharp comments designed to tug at the heartstrings. She didn't care if pressing was impertinent or rude. It was life or death, and there was no time for social niceties.

"You know this was murder," Rosemary said quietly.

With a resigned sigh, Miss McCoy said, "Yes, you're right. I know Dolph was murdered. I knew it the moment you told me about the electrical wires." Her mask slipped, the fight drained out of her, and she was no longer the haughty bestselling author. She was just a grieving woman—one scared for her own safety.

In as gentle a tone as she could muster, Rosemary asked, "How did you know, and why did you lie?"

"Because the way Dolph died is exactly like the murder was meant to happen in my next novel."

Rosemary's brow drew together skeptically. "The victim would be electrocuted with a rewired lamp and a

224

pilfered silver tea tray while aboard a transatlantic ocean liner?"

The author waved a hand. "Perhaps not precisely in that manner, but electrocuted, yes—close enough for me to know the means of murder wasn't a coincidence."

"Why, then, did you jump to the conclusion of a crazed fan?" Rosemary prodded. She needed to understand.

"Dolph's notebook, of course. He thought he'd lost it, but when he turned up dead, I realized it must have been stolen, and the contents used to kill him in the very same way we'd planned to kill the author in the book. Who else would do such a thing besides a deranged lunatic?"

Rosemary remembered Miss McCoy's instinctual reaction to the news. "And Hattie seemed to fit the bill since she's been asking so many questions about your work," she surmised. "I just don't understand why you would lie. Obviously, the murderer—be it Hattie or another individual—is still on board. They removed all evidence of the crime and probably tried to kill you with that bag of ball bearings. Why not tell the captain what you know?"

"To protect my career, of course!" Miss McCoy exclaimed as if it were the most natural conclusion at which to have arrived. "Do you know how difficult it is for a woman to find success as a writer? Have you any idea how many manuscripts I've had rejected? This was the first one I'd had Dolph. You know, some writers have excellent ideas but no drive or execution; others have the latter in spades but lack the creativity necessary to capture an audience. Those who can do both are the most successful. It's been a steep hill to climb, and now, I suspect, I'll begin a swift descent back to the bottom. I certainly couldn't turn in the story if word got out that that's how Dolph had died. The press would eat me alive if they found out I'd profited from my secretary's death."

If Miss McCoy's admission caused her to drop in Rosemary's estimation, it couldn't be helped. Finding Dolph's killer was the important thing. The author's next sentence put the final nail in the coffin of Rosemary's respect.

"The killer did not return to remove the tea tray." Miss McCoy fluttered a hand. "Because I'd already done so. The captain seemed quite content to accept a verdict of death by means of poor health, and as not having the true cause of death revealed was of utmost importance to me, I chose—quite wrongly, I suppose—to obfuscate."

Obfuscate. Fueled by fury, the word reverberated through Rosemary's mind. "You're aware that you could be brought up on charges of tampering with evidence, and your *obfuscation* has prompted the captain to think I'm a nuisance for insisting the death wasn't natural."

Fire blazed behind the author's eyes. "What happened

to *keeping secrets*?"

Rosemary met the fire with a narrow gaze. "I have no intention of telling on you. It wouldn't matter now, anyway. I merely need to understand what possible motive you could have for covering up a murder you didn't commit."

"As I said before, this trip was part research. It was also supposed to serve as an American tour to drum up interest in the *Poisoned Pen* in the hope of securing the success of my next book."

Now that Trix McCoy was talking, Rosemary clammed up and let the story come out. Besides, she was annoyed enough not to trust herself to speak.

"It looks bad enough to have planned a death exactly like Dolph's, but he had the whole scheme written down in his notebook, and since I don't know where that is now, I can only imagine what's to become of it. The murderer could easily publish it, and I'd be hanged for Dolph's murder myself! The only way to salvage my career is to get off this ship as quietly as possible and start back at square one. Or, perhaps, not at square one. I did find another of Dolph's notebooks in the pocket of his suitcase, so all is not lost."

Except for a man's life, but why bring up that trivial question? Rosemary thought incredulously.

She steeled her face into a neutral expression and asked, "Who else knew about the book's plot?" Because if no one else did, Miss McCoy was the only person with knowledge of the murder method. By that logic, she had to be either the killer or the intended victim.

Sorrow furrowed the author's brow. "I don't know, but Dolph must have mentioned it to someone." Speculation replaced grief. "Quite unprofessional of him, wasn't it?"

"I suppose so, and he never mentioned seeing anyone on board that he'd known from before the voyage?"

Shaking her head, Miss McCoy said sadly, "He didn't talk about himself much. I don't know much about his family apart from that they live in Devon. If he had friends, he never mentioned them, but he occasionally spoke of a former employer. Another author—aspiring, mind you, as I think none of the books were ever published."

Miss McCoy leaned forward conspiratorially. "Between you and me, Dolph said some unflattering things about the man. Called him a wet blanket—a pedant, if you will. Other than that, I'm afraid I have nothing useful to add to the investigation. I tend to lose myself in my work, and I've become quite adept at tuning out the rest of the world. Dolph may have said something of interest, but if he did, I have no recollection."

Pressing for more answers seemed futile. Instead, Rosemary excused herself, then closed Miss McCoy's stateroom door behind herself and leaned back against it with relief. It was difficult to understand how someone could value their career over their life. Perhaps the author was sick with grief, unable to think clearly. Or, perhaps she was simply batty!

Despite her admission that the murder method made her the most likely suspect, Miss McCoy had dropped all the way to the bottom of the list. She'd gained nothing from Dolph's death and, therefore, had no motive.

And wasn't the lack of motive the crux of the matter? There'd hardly been time enough to get on the wrong side of another passenger to the point where murder seemed like the only alternative. Unless Dolph had stumbled on the smuggling operation and Jimmy and Tony's big bad boss decided he had to die.

Other than that, there was no clear motive that Rosemary could see, which put her right back where she'd started before Miss McCoy had admitted her part in the proceedings.

Rosemary thought back to all the luggage stowed in the first-class cargo hold. Part of her wished she had given in to baser instincts and rummaged through everyone's things.

Perhaps Dolph's killer would be locked safely in the brig if she'd had fewer scruples. Of course, she would have had to know about the notebook in order to search for it. If only Trix McCoy had come clean earlier, she thought, and then tamped down her irritation. Nothing would change the past now and becoming frustrated wouldn't help matters.

Much of the compartment had yet to rouse, but Rosemary noticed Molly standing near one of the steward's trolleys at the station across the way.

"Do you know where this came from?" Stratford asked Molly, holding something up for her to see. "It was on my trolley," he said, sounding bewildered.

Molly's eyebrows drew together. "What is that?"

The object in Stratford's hand looked something like a pair of pliers but with a sharp edge instead of a blunt one. Rosemary didn't know what it was any more than Molly did. Then Stratford explained. "It's a pair of wire cutters, the type used for electrical work."

"I've no idea if they're not yours," Molly replied, her voice a squeak.

Stratford shook his head. "I've never used anything like this. Perhaps one of the other stewards left these here, but I can't imagine why."

"You know, that passenger who died . . ." Molly hedged.

"I've heard the rumors," Stratford replied, "but I didn't put any stock in them. It's absurd, isn't it?"

Molly shrugged. "Worse and more surprising things have happened, haven't they?"

"It *was* murder." Rosemary surprised herself along

with Stratford and Molly, and she realized she must have looked like a lunatic, popping into the alcove unannounced and obviously having been eavesdropping. "And that tool you're holding was probably used to strip the wires that ultimately killed Mr. Sutton. Would you like to explain yourself?"

Stratford continued to peer at Rosemary as though she were quite mad but also appeared to struggle with the correct response, given she was one of the first-class passengers he'd sworn to serve to the highest level of satisfaction.

"I've nothing to explain, madam," Stratford said politely. "I've never seen these before, and furthermore, what reason would I have to murder a passenger? Dead men don't tip, do they?"

Rosemary could think of a few reasons why Mr. Sutton might have been a liability for the steward. Perhaps Dolph had overheard or seen something he wasn't supposed to. Maybe he knew that Stratford was the boss Jimmy and Tony hadn't wanted to cross and had to be silenced. She didn't much care about the *why* only that justice be served.

"They also don't talk," she said. "What might Mr. Sutton have discovered that would put him in harm's way?"

"I'm afraid that I would have absolutely no idea. I'm grateful to have a job that, erm, pays well, shall we say."

"The question is," Rosemary spoke her thoughts, possibly unwisely, "whether your discretion can be purchased by the unscrupulous."

CHAPTER TWENTY-SIX

The new plot to bring down the duplicitous Parsons couple had come together far easier than expected once the group had decided, at Rosemary's suggestion, that if they couldn't get them by trick, they'd get them by force.

After lunch, she, Desmond, and Mr. Tait bade Vera and Frederick good luck and then took the lift up to the Promenade Deck to set their part of the plan in motion.

"Sadie." Desmond caught the attention of one of the young women watching a shuffleboard match with some interest and the men participating in it with far more. She broke away from her friends and approached Desmond who, after a brief explanation smiled hopefully. "I wonder if I might prevail upon you for a bit of assistance."

Keeping his speech formal didn't seem to deter the hope that rose in Sadie's eyes, but Desmond pressed on and explained the situation.

"If you'd be willing to round up those of the first-class passengers who have fallen foul of those rogues, it would help our cause immensely."

Owing Desmond for helping her out of a jam, Sadie agreed without hesitation and toddled off to enlist the help of her friends. When she'd gone, Rosemary turned to him.

"*Fallen foul of those rogues*?" she teased. "You sound like my father when he's at his most pedantic."

"Oh, leave it off, Rosie." Desmond's face flushed. "I'm trying to make an impression."

"Well, I think it's a brilliant scheme." Mr. Tait glanced at Desmond admiringly. To Rosemary, he said, "I like this lad," and winked. "We'll canvass the men's smoking room for those enjoying a nice Cuban after their midday meal and see you ladies later, down below."

Mr. Tait, usually rather pompous, was quite enjoying himself, Rosemary thought with a smile. She supposed the notion of foiling the Parsons was sufficiently pleasant to have roused his spirits; it had certainly roused hers. The plan was simplicity itself, and Rosemary only wished they'd thought of it sooner.

Later, she and Mr. Tait took their places in the same cluster of armchairs where they'd sat the evening when Mrs. Long lost at bridge (and the night Dolph Sutton was murdered, neither had forgotten) and waited patiently.

Each fortified with a double shot of brandy to calm their nerves, the Longs sat on the other side of the palm fronds at one of the tables generally reserved for bridge and pretended to enjoy a cup of tea. Rosemary only hoped they could tamp down their anger and frustration long enough to allow events to play out as planned.

"Be patient, please," Desmond advised from his post.

It wasn't long before Frederick and Vera, their spirits quite high indeed, entered the Winter Garden Lounge with Mr. And Mrs. Parsons on their tail. The couple appeared at ease for once, which was unsurprising, at least to Rosemary, though she realized it shouldn't have been. Frederick and Vera alone possessed an above-average amount of gravitas; together, they were an ineffable force.

"It's the last night, and I simply can't abide having lost nearly every wager I've made!" Frederick boomed, his voice slurring slightly as though he'd consumed one too many G&Ts. "At least let me try to make my money back," he cajoled.

To the casual observer, Mrs. Parsons would have shown little interest, but Rosemary saw her eyes flash greedily. Her husband didn't follow suit until Frederick added in challenge, "Unless you're afraid of a high-stakes match? One round, winner takes all?"

Mr. Parsons didn't flinch. He appraised Frederick,

from the cut of his custom-tailored suit to the diamond-studded cuff links to the supple leather of Italian shoes, finally settling on his face, which had been arranged into a leisurely, devil-may-care expression.

If it had been a ring fight, Mr. Parsons would have flexed his muscles and thrown a practice punch. Instead, he said, "I've nothing to fear, Mr. Woolridge. You've got yourself a match," and extended his hand towards Frederick.

"Not so fast, old chap," Frederick said in the same jovial tone he'd been using, except with a slightly sharper edge. "I'll be asking my friend Des to stand in. Me, I don't know a thing about the game. Is that a problem?" There was no longer so much as a trace of a slur in his voice.

It almost seemed that Mr. Parsons was going to back out, but he looked around and noted that the raised voices appeared to have caused quite a flurry. Several passengers now looked on with avid interest.

"No problem at all." Mr. Parsons shrugged, pasted a serene smile on his face, and shook Desmond's hand instead of Frederick's. "I'm happy to take money from either one of you," he said with a smug smile.

Desmond merely raised an eyebrow, and then it was on. Quickly, the table was set and readied, and the Parsons took their seats at north and south, with Desmond and Vera representing east and west.

Since Frederick had no understanding of the game or what everyone was waiting on tenterhooks for, Rosemary explained in a low voice, "There are thirteen rounds or "tricks," and whoever wins the most tricks—by playing the highest card—wins. It's during the bidding round that the Parsons will set their trap."

Vera dealt the first hand, and as Rosemary had explained, the bidding began.

"One diamond," said Mr. Parsons and pushed his cigarette case towards his partner. Some of the passengers who had begun to observe the game paid special attention to the case, but the Parsons were so wrapped up with their cards neither of them seemed to notice.

Desmond bid two hearts, and then Mrs. Parsons three, after which Vera announced, "Two spades."

During Mr. Parsons' next bid, he picked up his cigarette case and shook it, almost absentmindedly, three times. With each bid, Frederick appeared more and more confused.

"Mr. Parsons signaled on a bid of diamonds," Rosemary whispered, "and then again when he bid spades. It's a code, so Mrs. Parsons can tell which cards he has in those suits. It's rather complicated and actually quite genius," she said, almost sounding impressed. "If they make a move that doesn't seem at all sensible and still win, this crowd will know exactly what they're up to."

"How do you tell if a move isn't sensible?" Frederick wanted to know.

Rosemary sighed, "As mother always says, bridge takes a day to teach and a lifetime to master, Freddie. I couldn't possibly explain it to you in a matter of minutes."

Finally, Desmond won the round on a designed bid of five no trump, and the match began.

"Five is a high bid," Rosemary explained to Frederick. "You always have to add six, which means if the Parsons want to win the game, they have to take eleven of the thirteen tricks. Desmond and Vera are trying to make them slip up."

"Add six?" Frederick asked, confused again. Rosemary didn't bother to answer.

It took quite a few tricks before Mrs. Parsons led with a king of hearts even though the highest of that suit to have been played was a ten. Anyone could have had the ace, and she would have lost one of the tricks necessary for her and her partner to win the game. When she won the trick, the only explanation was that she had known Mr. Parsons held the ace.

Primed by Desmond's lady friends to keep an eye on the cigarette case, a goodly portion of the watching crowd had picked up on the signals as well. The accusations began as a buzz of whispering discussion, then rose to a roar.

When Mrs. Parsons heard the words *cheating* and *cigarette case* cast in her husband's direction, she blanched.

"You set us up!" Mr. Parsons growled out the accusation as he glared first at Frederick and then Desmond. "You no-good swindler!"

"That's rich, coming from you," Desmond retorted and sat back in his chair to appraise Mr. Parsons and his wife. The smile on his face should have been warning enough, but Mr. Parsons didn't sense that he'd begun to tread into dangerous waters.

Mr. Parsons scoffed. "If you didn't want to lose, you shouldn't have taken the wager to begin with, and besides, you're traveling first class—you can afford it." The last statement came out sounding more bitter than black coffee.

Unable to maintain his composure, Mr. Long stood and shouted, "Not everyone traveling first-class can afford to lose money, you louse!"

"Nor should they be expected to," said one of the gentlemen who had been crowded around the palm fronds, watching along with Rosemary and Desmond.

The Parsons had not expected to be descended upon by half the people whose money they had swindled from them, and the panicked expressions on their faces caused Rosemary an intense feeling of satisfaction. Her plan had worked; it had been executed perfectly by her friends, and it looked as though justice for the Long couple might actually be served.

"You have a problem with first-class passengers?" asked another bystander, a large, mustachioed American man whose snarl indicated there was only one answer to that question.

One more stepped forward and commented, "You sure seem to enjoy the money you've fleeced us for. That's called hypocrisy."

Suddenly, the Winter Garden Lounge seemed much smaller than before and the crowd rather larger. Mrs. Parsons must have felt the pinch of her mistakes closing in because she looked at her husband with wide, almost feral eyes that flicked suggestively towards the exit.

Mr. Mustache grabbed Mr. Parsons by the arm and dragged the man bodily from his chair. When Mr. Parsons attempted to break free, he found himself in a firm grip, his toes just barely touching the floor, nose to nose with the angry American.

"Put me down," Mr. Parsons ordered with very little conviction.

"I'd like to *put you down*, but murder is a crime," the American all but growled. Rosemary wished she knew his name but continued to call him Mr. Mustache in her head. "And if cheating good people out of their money and possessions isn't a crime, it should be. It's as good as stealing."

"Throw him overboard." someone, Rosemary couldn't see who, shouted from the rear of the crowd, and within seconds, more voices joined in to chant the same.

Since actual murder wasn't part of the plan, Frederick and Desmond found themselves in the unenviable position of defending the man who had cheated them.

"Let's not be hasty, shall we." Frederick stepped forward and rested his hand on the wrist of the man still holding Mr. Parsons just as Mrs. Parsons began to wail.

"We're sorry. Please, don't kill my husband. We'll give you your money back. All of it. Everything we took."

Mr. Mustache kept hold of Mr. Parsons but turned his head to cast a gaze over the assemblage. "What do you say? Shall we accept restitution?"

When the general answer was yes, Rosemary let out the breath she'd been holding, then realized she needn't have worried when Mr. Mustache caught her eye and offered a wink. Since his scare tactic had worked a treat, Rosemary responded in kind and made a note to thank him later.

The Longs were the first to receive restitution and left the Parsons' stateroom with their moods greatly improved. The first thing Mr. Long did was to approach Frederick and offer his hand.

"How can I repay you for what you've done?" He

glanced past Frederick to include the rest of the group in his appreciation.

"We were happy to help." Frederick narrowed his eyes thoughtfully, "But there is one thing you could do. Follow me, please."

The two men left and, after a short time, returned with Mr. Long holding several comics, which he promised to read and then pass on to his son.

"That was a lovely thing you did," Rosemary said to Frederick a few moments later when she'd got him alone. "You'll make a wonderful father someday."

Chapter Twenty-Seven

Rosemary and her friends left a buoyant Mr. Tait in charge of returning the Parsons' ill-gotten gains to the first-class passengers. While the men enjoyed a cocktail, Rosemary helped Vera dress for dinner. She herself had chosen a very simple floor-length black frock in contrast to Vera's sensational haute couture piece.

"You're positively smashing," Rosemary assured her friend. "Mirella Verratti has nothing on you, Vera dear."

At the mention of the singer, Vera frowned. "What a disappointment that whole debacle turned out to be. I've barely spoken three words to her in the last five days, and somehow I've managed to look like a complete dolt at every opportunity. Perhaps I'm not destined for stardom after all if I can still become starstruck myself!"

Balking, Rosemary said, "You're human, Vera, don't forget."

Vera let out a swift exhale of breath and appraised herself in the mirror once more. "Don't remind me. I just want tonight to be perfect," she said, adjusting her headpiece into a more secure position. "Are you ready?"

The sound of a bugle rent the air, signaling that dinner would commence in fifteen minutes. "I suppose I have to be, don't I?" Rosemary replied.

If possible, the grand descent was an even bigger spectacle than on the first evening aboard. Then, it had been about first impressions, about presenting oneself as a member of the exclusive society set. This night, however, was about *lasting* impressions.

And oh, what an impression Vera made! Her dress, a true piece of art, was sleeveless white with a sheer black overlay, at least three inches of fringe around the hem, and a plunging neckline. She wore elbow-length black gloves, a diamond-encrusted headband over a mass of finger curls, and a long string of pearls wrapped thrice around her head.

Frederick, who truly adored his stunning wife, even wore the monocle she'd bought him, discovering quite conveniently that it was excellent for reading the dinner menu's tiny print. "Thank goodness I've dodged a bullet—no snails or entrails for me tonight," he said with a grin.

Miss McCoy had rallied, and she now sat next to Mr. Tait. The man had even escorted her down the stairs, and Rosemary suspected he must still be riding high from foiling the cheating Parsons.

Hattie maneuvered herself into a seat on the other side of Miss McCoy and only pouted a little bit when she discovered everyone else had been on quite an adventure without her.

Even Mr. and Mrs. Long appeared rather content and, in fact, five years younger, wearing smiles rather than the perpetual frown that had graced both their faces for most of the journey.

It was almost as if Dolph's death, the discovery of the smuggled rum, and the attempt to harm Miss McCoy had never happened. Except Rosemary hadn't forgotten, and she also hadn't stopped puzzling over the clues. Time was running out; within eighteen hours, the ship would dock in New York, and a killer would walk free.

She still had the case of diamonds and cash locked away with the purser, and without any proof the goods were stolen, she would soon be forced to either hand it over to the captain or back to Hattie herself.

It looked like perhaps, for the first time, she might not come out of an investigation victorious, and she didn't like the thought of that one bit.

"Everyone is simply abuzz with excitement for the Verrattis' performance. It seems they've become even more of a sensation since their public breakup than before," Vera commented incredulously after the first course of oysters on the half shell had been delivered to the table.

"It's the nature of celebrity," Miss McCoy replied, daintily dabbing her napkin to the corner of her mouth. "They'll sell even more records now, mark my words."

Desmond handed his dinner menu to Mr. Tait during the lull between courses and said, "I'd very much like your address. Perhaps we can get together either in New York or back in London." It seemed that not only had Mr. Tait taken a shine to Desmond, but the feeling was also mutual.

At his question, menus began to be handed around, along with Mr. Tait's pen, he having been the only one of the group to think to bring one along. "Does this outfit look as though it has pockets?" Vera asked her husband with a laugh. "What's your excuse, dear?"

Rosemary finished signing her name on her companions' menus and had been handed hers back when the clinking of glass caught her attention. A familiar-looking young man took the stage, and when he began to speak into the microphone, Rosemary tucked the menu into her minuscule handbag and regarded him more closely.

"Sorry to interrupt your dinner, but I have an announcement to make, and it simply can't wait." The man reached into his pocket to fish around for something, and when he turned his head, she remembered where she'd seen him before: in the shops purchasing a diamond engagement ring.

How strange for her holiday to be bookended by marriage proposals: first Anna, and now some lucky young lady who was probably swooning over her beau and his public display of affection. "Audrey, my love, will you marry me?" the young man asked confidently.

A pretty young girl at the table where he'd been sitting stood up uncertainly, and Rosemary's heart fluttered. She recognized the would-be bride as the one who had been listening so intently to Mirella Verratti's advice the previous day in the hair salon.

Rosemary looked around for the singer, who had declined to make a grand entrance but was sitting awkwardly between her soon-to-be ex-husband and the journalist covering their holiday. Mrs. Verratti watched the two young people, her eyes wide and her lips pursed together in expectation.

"No, I'm sorry, I can't. You're simply . . . not the one!" the girl said, and Rosemary watched both her beau and Mrs. Verratti's faces crumple. Mrs. Verratti recovered quickly, but it didn't make much difference since nobody else's eyes were on her.

"Audrey, wait," the young man called, running after the girl. Immediately, the band resumed playing, this time a much jauntier tune, as if attempting to elevate the mood with sheer rhythm alone.

"Well, I say!" Miss McCoy exclaimed. "That's the end of the evening for me. I think I'll retire to my stateroom now."

"But, Miss McCoy," Hattie protested, "you'll miss the Verrattis' performance! It's sure to be even more intriguing now that they are at loggerheads, don't you think?"

The author shrugged. "You'll describe it to me over breakfast, our last meal together. I do hope to see you all then." She directed warm glances around the table before taking her leave.

Vera watched her go and said, "I wonder what sort of drugs Molly's got her on to make her so pleasant."

Mr. Tait's lip twitched as though he might smile, but Rosemary admonished her friend. "She's lost someone she cared for deeply, Vera. Don't be glib. Perhaps she's feeling a rare moment of relief from the pain of it."

"Or she's happy we've all but docked and she's got away with his murder," Vera retorted, causing Mr. Tait to look in her direction. He, evidently, wasn't the least bit hard of hearing.

Rosemary brushed off Vera's comment. She felt quite certain that Trix McCoy had been telling the truth; she was innocent, there was little doubt in Rosemary's mind. "She's probably just happy she found more of Dolph's notes tucked away in one of his cases," she rationalized.

"You tend to give people the benefit of the doubt, Rosie, even when you shouldn't. You're far too trusting," Vera replied. "It's one of your best and worst qualities all in one."

Balking, Rosemary fired back, "Withholding condemnation until all the facts have been revealed isn't being too trusting. I'm simply unwilling to jump to conclusions, that's all."

"And that's why you're the best of us, Rosie."

For some reason, Vera's faith in her character chafed. Did she deserve such a title? Did she even want it? Too many questions began crowding her mind, so Rosemary excused herself to the powder room.

Partway there, a flash of pink pulled Rosemary's eye towards a large potted palm and caused her to take a detour.

"Rose, sweetie," she admonished lightly, "what are you doing down here? You're supposed to be in bed."

The little girl held out the notebook with the sketch she'd been working on. With an economy of line, she'd captured the essence of the grand staircase, the elegant flourish of a feathered headband, the sleek lines of a black suit coat, the shine of pearls under a chandelier.

"I had to see, and when I saw, I had to draw," the little girl said simply. "Please don't tell my mother. I just had to come."

"I understand." Because she did, and all too well, Rosemary laid a hand on the little girl's head. "May I look?" Gently, she accepted the notebook and flipped back a page, her eyes widening as she saw both Vera and herself portrayed in pencil.

The next page showed Mr. and Mrs. Parsons sitting alone, their expressions carefully blank. The fact that they'd shown those faces at all was a surprise to Rosemary, and when she peered between the palm fronds, it was to find they'd left the dining room already.

"He's very angry," said little Rose. "See there." She pointed to the faint lines she'd added around his mouth. "And it's all her fault, he says."

From her vantage point, the girl couldn't possibly have heard Mr. Parsons speak.

"How do you know?"

"My father showed me how to tell what people are saying by watching how they move their lips. That lady said she was sorry, but she didn't mean it. They're both angry, I think. But not as angry as that other man."

Quickly, Rosemary flipped through more drawings but saw none that showed the mysterious *other man*.

"Which man?"

"I can't remember his name, but he was sitting next to that really tall lady who just left."

Trix McCoy.

"Mr. Tait?" Rosemary asked, her voice a squeak. "Was he angry with Miss McCoy?"

Rose shook her head solemnly. "No. With the man who died."

Mr. Tait had argued with Dolph Sutton? The news hit

Rosemary like a ton of bricks. "When?" she asked warily. "Where?"

"The day before he died, in the corridor by his room," Rose answered. "He was swapping rooms with the tall lady, and I could see them from the common room.

When Rosemary frowned, the child seemed worried. "Have I done something wrong?"

"No, dear. Of course not," Rosemary reassured. "Can you tell me what the two men were arguing about?"

Again, Rose shook her head solemnly. "I couldn't see well enough."

What could it mean? Rosemary wondered as she sent little Rose back off to B Deck and her bed. Her need for the powder room had become quite urgent indeed, however, and the queue was quite long, so she took the stairs up one level to the open section of C Deck overlooking the dining hall and finally found a deserted restroom.

She splashed some cold water onto her face, touched up her lipstick, and tried to settle her nerves, all the while wondering what exactly had been the content of the argument between Dolph and Mr. Tait. Did it have to do with Dolph's death, or was it simply a minor disagreement over something innocuous, such as Miss McCoy's inability to sleep without utter silence?

On her way back to her table, Rosemary stopped at the place where little Rose had been hidden, crouched to look between the fronds, and committed what she saw to memory. As she stood, she heard dulcet tones speaking in Italian.

Just on the other side of the greenery, Mrs. Verratti stood with the poor lad who'd just had his proposal go down in flames in front of the entire assemblage. Over his lowered head, the singer caught Rosemary's eye, and the two women shared a look of pity for the boy.

"*Il primo amore non si scorda mai.*" Mirella Verratti told him, then repeated the phrase in English. "The first love is never forgotten, but do not despair. *Lontano dagli occhi, lontano dal cuore.*"

Out of sight, out of mind. Probably not the worst advice one could give to the lovelorn, especially not when combined with an offer to introduce the lad to someone who might better suit him. Whether the boy appreciated the offer, Rosemary would not get the chance to learn.

A hand closed around her arm, and Rosemary started—more than started actually—and whipped around to find herself face-to-face with Captain Hughes.

"Mrs. Lillywhite," the captain said before she could ask what precisely it was he thought he was doing. "You need to come with us. Now." The expression on his face brooked no refusal.

"What? Why? Go with you where?" Rosemary demanded indignantly.

252

Captain Hughes' eyes pierced hers. "I think you know why, Mrs. Lillywhite. It's been brought to my attention that you've helped yourself to the key to the first-class cargo hold. And of course, there's also the rum."

"The rum?" Rosemary's heart threatened to beat out of her chest. The captain turned and picked up a suitcase she hadn't noticed—her suitcase, the one she'd been missing since she boarded the ship! "Where did you get that?" she exclaimed.

He didn't answer her question and instead said, "Mrs. Lillywhite, I'm afraid I'm going to have to detain you."

"Detain me?" Rosemary sputtered, planting her feet and peering over the edge of the railing to the dining saloon below. Her friends, unfortunately, were all otherwise occupied, none of them looking in her direction.

"Yes, Mrs. Lillywhite. In the brig," the captain said gravely and guided her towards the lifts. Instead of boarding, he went around the other side of the grand staircase, to a short, almost hidden corridor packed with stacks of supplies for the evening's celebration, and into a stairwell Rosemary recognized as one designated for staff. It had the same color walls and trim as the one she had used to escape Jimmy and Tony two evenings prior.

Down they climbed to the E Deck, where Rosemary vaguely recalled some of the staff quarters were located.

"In here, Mrs. Lillywhite," the captain said. She was

almost disappointed to discover that the brig, which she'd envisioned as a jail cell for unruly passengers, was actually just an unused steward's berth with a couple of uncomfortable chairs in place of the bed. There was also a desk, behind which sat a bored-looking steward who perked right to attention when the captain made his entrance.

"Sir," he said with deference and received a short nod in response.

When they were inside, and she'd taken a seat, the captain put the case on the table and opened it up, spinning it around for dramatic effect so Rosemary could see what was inside.

"That's not mine," she said when she saw that the suitcase contained several bottles of familiar-looking rum. She opened her mouth to tell the captain about the coffins in the first-class cargo hold but stopped short. Surely, if someone had filled this case with it, they'd made an effort to hide the rest.

If she sent the captain on a wild goose chase, he would never believe her anything but guilty. Oh, how she wished she'd just told him about the coffins, to begin with!

"You see, Mrs. Lillywhite, I'm quite a sleuth myself, and I know you're not being truthful," the captain said.

Exasperated, Rosemary called on her patience. "I reported that suitcase missing days ago. One of the stewards delivered a similar one to my room, and it had a bottle of the same kind of rum inside. You need to go and find a Miss Hattie Humphries in the first-class dining saloon," she instructed. "It was her suitcase."

"That's rather interesting," the captain replied, "considering she's the one who found this suitcase—*your* suitcase—and turned you in."

Before Rosemary could form a reply, the telephone on the wall near the desk trilled, and the steward scrambled to answer it.

"Yes, yes, of course. Captain," he said, hanging up the receiver. "It's control. You're needed up top, as soon as possible."

The captain sighed and seemed to consider for a moment before stalking towards the door. "Keep an eye on her until I get back," he commanded over his shoulder.

Chapter Twenty-Eight

"This is absurd," Rosemary complained once the captain had gone. "Do I really look like a rum smuggler to you?"

She tried to talk some sense into the steward, all the while thinking about Hattie and wondering how she'd known Rosemary had the suitcase in the first place and why, if she'd wanted it back, had she simply not asked for it? Surely, this—setting her up with the ship's captain—was much more trouble? Could she have been coerced into doing so?

The steward nodded apologetically. "I'm sure you're not, madam, but unfortunately, I can't disobey my captain's orders."

Outside in the corridor, someone walked past the door. Rosemary caught the motion in her peripheral vision and heard the noise of swishing fabric but didn't see who it was.

She lowered her voice and, changing tactics,

implored, "The real criminals will get away with it if you continue to focus on me. I can help." Rosemary's earlier fear of the evidence being disposed of gave way to an even graver one where she was convicted of a crime she hadn't committed. "They've got a whole coffin full of rum down in the cargo hold!"

The steward scoffed, her words falling on deaf ears— or so she thought, until the same swishing noise she had heard before preceded Mirella Verratti through the door. "Oh, there you are," she said, shooting Rosemary a friendly but admonishing look. "I've been searching everywhere for you, and then I was told you'd been carted off by the captain himself! Honestly, you're always getting yourself into some sort of scrape, aren't you, *mia amica*? Come along now; we shall be late. *Sbrigati*."

The steward swallowed hard and stared at Mrs. Verratti almost as incredulously as Rosemary.

Not needing to be told twice to hurry up, Rosemary stood, then stopped when the steward hastened to stand in front of the door.

"I can't let her leave," he said. "The captain said."

"I haven't done anything wrong," Rosemary defended herself.

"*Certamente.*" Mrs. Verratti sighed. "I suppose I must respect the captain's wishes."

Rosemary's heart dropped to her feet, along with her

hopes of being freed.

"You," Mrs. Verratti said and crooked a finger at the steward. His throat worked as he swallowed hard, twice. "Must come and show me how to get back to the Grand Saloon. I'm afraid I've become . . . what is the word . . . mixed up? I cannot be sure if I will find my way back."

Relief washed over the steward's face as he hastened to explain how to navigate the passageways that would lead her back to where she belonged. Then, Mrs. Verratti repeated his instructions, making several mistakes and becoming visibly frustrated.

"Could you not just show me?" How any man could resist the perfect pout of her lips or the plea in Mirella Verratti's eyes, Rosemary didn't know.

The steward held out for mere seconds. "Yes. Let me just get the key." He turned to Rosemary. "I'm sorry, I'll have to lock you in."

It wasn't that Rosemary envied women like Vera and Mrs. Verratti their skill for washing all rational thought from a man's mind with nothing more than a sidelong look . . . or was it? Maybe only at times like these.

On her way out, Mrs. Verratti tossed Rosemary a wink and a nod. As soon as the door swung closed, Rosemary slumped in her seat. Her daring escape had not gone to plan. Not that there had been an actual plan or a daring escape in the first place, but even so, her

258

hopes felt dashed.

Two seconds later, the high trill of female laughter echoed through the door, followed by a scraping sound, and the key slid under the door. Rosemary realized that, perhaps, plans didn't matter—not when feminine wiles came into play!

She snatched up the key, waited a few seconds, and opened the door, sidling into the corridor. Conscious that she needed to get far away before the steward returned, Rosemary turned and headed in the opposite direction.

While she needed to get back upstairs, she didn't know where Captain Hughes might be. He'd gone up top and could be making his way back to E Deck at any moment. Meeting him on the stairs was not something she considered wise, so she took them down instead.

Between the E and G Deck staircases, Rosemary rather serendipitously found Molly, looking quite frazzled and as though she needed a proper break. "Molly! Thank goodness!" Rosemary realized too late she probably looked like a lunatic. "Go and get my friends, please," she implored. "They're in the dining room. Mr. and Mrs. Woolridge and Mr. Cooper. Tell them to hurry to the first-class cargo hold. My brother will know what to do."

Molly was only able to nod, her mouth agape, but Rosemary took it as confirmation the task would be completed and continued down the last flight of stairs.

When she arrived at the entrance to the cargo hold, the door was open—just a crack, but enough for her to know someone was inside. A shuffling noise and a muffled shout were emitted from the crack, and Rosemary only needed two guesses as to who was banging around in there.

She had meant it when she'd told Frederick she wasn't sure what Jimmy and Tony might have done if she'd been caught listening to their previous conversation outside that very same door. Her heart began to race, and she considered turning back, but for some reason, the message didn't seem to reach from her brain all the way to her feet.

They propelled her forward instead of backward, her feet and the visceral need to see the story through to its conclusion. Perhaps she could, as she'd already done several times before, glean some bit of information by staying quiet and listening—at least until her brother and friends arrived to act as reinforcements.

With that thought in mind, Rosemary sneaked into the hold with its series of cages denoting the compartments above and crouched down low. She ducked into one of the sections near to the door and positioned herself behind a pile of trunks.

"It's not here, Tony, I'm tellin' ya." Rosemary recognized Jimmy's squeaky voice—would recognize it anywhere, she suspected, it having been seared into her brain. "Why do we have to come all the way back down here to scour the place when we've already thoroughly searched it?"

The two thugs were at the opposite end of the hold, but by some feat of or perhaps an error in engineering, their voices echoed and sounded almost as though they were standing right behind Rosemary. The hairs on the back of her neck stood to attention, but she took some comfort in knowing they weren't as close as they seemed.

Tony grunted, and the sound of a large piece of luggage being moved around echoed across the space. "Because that's what we were told to do, Jimbo," he replied, his tone indicating Jimmy ought not to ask too many more questions.

When another noise, this time a scrape, sounded from behind her, Rosemary didn't flinch, assuming it had come from where her eyes were trained. She did, however, react a moment later when a throat cleared, and she realized she'd miscalculated the direction of the sound.

Her blood ran cold, and then she felt a flood of relief when she realized it was only Hattie Humphries standing behind her.

The relief didn't last for long because the young woman's eyes weren't filled with fear or even hesitation when she commanded Rosemary, "Stand up, Mrs.

Lillywhite," in a voice loud enough to alert Jimmy and Tony of her presence.

"Who's she?" Tony demanded when he'd caught sight of Rosemary. "What's she doing down here?"

"Snooping," Hattie replied in a tone that dripped acid. "She does that a lot."

Three against one. Long odds of getting away. Better to keep Hattie talking until help arrived. Trying for a conversational tone rather than a confrontational one, Rosemary said, "Interesting choice for running a smuggling operation," and hoped the expression on her face didn't betray her.

"What safer place than first-class for maneuvering past security?" Hattie asked. "Just like on land, wealthy and connected passengers can get away with anything— including murder, it seems," she scoffed. "Though had I known what sort of trouble I was in for, I would have chosen a stateroom on the Shelter Deck instead."

Rosemary's eyes narrowed at her use of the term Shelter Deck. It wasn't one with which she was familiar; she hadn't even heard it in passing during her time on board. From the context, she extrapolated that Hattie was referring to C Deck, where the rest of the first-class accommodations were located.

"You're not quite as empty-headed as you come across, are you, Hattie?" Rosemary asked, taking a step back instinctively.

"You all simply assumed I didn't know my way around, and I let you believe what you wanted to believe," Hattie replied with a shrug. "Playing the thickhead always works. Nobody expects much more from a pretty young woman."

Some men did. Max, for instance, but Hattie's boss probably wasn't as forward-thinking. Rosemary remembered the trinket box that she'd found alongside the diamonds. Could it belong to one of the staff members? "Who are you smuggling the rum for?"

Jimmy, whose eyes had been volleying back and forth between Rosemary and Hattie, exclaimed, "Hey, how does she know about the rum?"

"Tell me who your boss is," Rosemary asked again, "and we can go to the captain together and turn him in. Is it the steward Stratford? Was it his lapel pin in your suitcase?" It occurred to her only too late that perhaps Hattie and Stratford were doing more than working together, and if that were the case, Rosemary realized, she might be in more trouble than she'd thought.

Hattie scoffed again and wiped that particular concern from Rosemary's mind. "Stratford the steward? Truly, do you believe that lout is capable of managing both his job and a smuggling operation simultaneously? I thought you were more intelligent than that, Mrs. Lillywhite. Why would he have delivered that case to your room if he knew it was mine?"

It was a good point, that, and one that Rosemary hadn't considered.

"This is your fault," Tony accused Hattie before Rosemary could wind up a retort. "You've exposed us. You got greedy and overplayed our hand. You couldn't stop at the rum; you had to go for the jewels, too. I knew we should have figured one of those coffins would need to be used at some point."

Rosemary was surprised to discover that Tony thought about much at all, but then again, he had seemed like the brighter of the pair—marginally so, but enough to count, evidently.

"We're all greedy, Tony," Hattie retorted. "We're all in it for the money, certainly not for the fun—at least not all of us." She cast a derisive glance at her two counterparts, and that was when Rosemary realized the big boss wasn't some mysterious, burly man. The big boss wasn't a man at all. It was Hattie!

Rosemary recalled her dismissal of Trix McCoy's comment regarding Hattie's possible involvement in Dolph's death. The idea had been so ludicrous that she had immediately laughed it off, thinking all the while that wouldn't it be just the twist for what was turning out to be a mystery-themed trip across the Atlantic? Poetic or not, she certainly hadn't wanted to be correct on that count.

"You were trying to get into my stateroom so you

could get the suitcase back," Rosemary realized with a shock. "And it was you, in the stairwell—or rather, one of these two." She gestured towards Jimmy and Tony. "Except they weren't aiming for Miss McCoy at all. They were aiming for me, at your instruction! You're the one who organized this whole operation!"

Hattie let loose an evil-sounding laugh. "Congratulations! You guessed correctly, Mrs. Lillywhite. That was almost a debacle. Miss McCoy had plenty of time to get up those stairs; at least, she ought to have had. Honestly, she really should think about losing some weight."

To Rosemary's mind, Miss McCoy's robustness felt like a blessing. Had she not been in the stairwell, Rosemary wouldn't have forced Vera to hang back, and the well-aimed bag of ball bearings might have struck its target!

"If all had gone according to plan, you'd be dead."

"And Miss McCoy? Were you trying to frame her or just drive her mad?"

Rosemary couldn't imagine what the author could have done to spark such hatred and came down in favor of the theory that Hattie was the mad one. Anger was one thing; hatred another—but as Rosemary had said before, it wasn't often crimes were committed in the absence of emotion. Not unless they were perpetrated by someone with no moral code. Hattie was the most dangerous kind of criminal because she didn't seem to feel she had anything to lose.

Hattie turned on Rosemary, her eyes flashing with the first genuine emotion she'd displayed. "It's a good thing you're still alive, however. That pin belonged to my father, and I want it back. I'm only going to ask you this once. Where is my suitcase now?"

Suddenly, it became apparent that Rosemary was in trouble—big trouble—and it didn't seem as though her friends were going to arrive in time to save her. Was it possible that Molly hadn't delivered her message? Perhaps she was in on the smuggling operation as well! Rosemary didn't think anything would surprise her anymore.

She began to back away in the direction of the door, but Hattie pointed a finger as though the two thugs were nothing more than hunting dogs and said, "Stop her," from between clenched teeth.

"We told you we didn't want no part in murder," Tony said, holding his hand in the air. "Bootleggin's one thing, but it ain't right, hurtin' a lady, and I won't do it again." Perhaps the thugs weren't entirely homicidal after all.

Rosemary fought to keep her hands from shaking, looking around to get a better handle on her surroundings. She glanced up towards the ceiling, and it was as though the heavens had opened just for her. In the air above Jimmy and Tony's heads, a load of suitcases dangled from the ceiling by a rope secured to a hook on the wall less than ten feet from where Rosemary stood.

Meanwhile, Hattie looked Tony square in the eyes and spat, "Just tie her up. Now," and it seemed to carry more weight than one word should have. Rosemary shivered at the question of what this unassuming woman had done to strike such fear.

For a few more charged seconds, Tony seemed to consider, looking between Rosemary and Hattie. While he debated with himself, Hattie became all the more agitated, and Rosemary took the opportunity to move closer to the hook.

"Oh, hell, I'll do it," Jimmy said, taking a step toward her. To his surprise, Rosemary lunged, which made him pause long enough for her to lift the rope from its hook.

Jimmy went down in a rain of suitcases, his muttered expletives letting Rosemary know she hadn't killed, only injured. She felt a quick flash of relief for that before she raced to the door, flung it open, and ran for freedom. Unfortunately, Tony had only received a glancing blow that shoved him sideways, and he followed close behind.

In the corridor, Rosemary made a mad dash for the stairs, managing to make it up one level before realizing they were gaining on her quickly. Instead of continuing up the steep staircase, she exited to F Deck and kept running.

Frantic, Rosemary remembered the food storage area from her last trip below decks; it had been filled with crates, cabinets, shelves, and cupboards—any number of places where a petite woman like herself could hide. However, when she got there, she realized where all the supplies now crowding the corridor off the Saloon Deck had come from.

With nowhere to hide and Hattie and Tony trailing, Rosemary ran through the double doors that led to the pool.

"Stop right there!" She heard Hattie's voice behind her. As if she had a choice! Her legs felt like rubber, and her lungs burned in the sudden stifling humidity. "Where is my suitcase?" Hattie thundered.

"It's in the safest place it could possibly be," Rosemary answered, attempting to stall on the off chance that help, in some form, might arrive. "The purser's safety deposit box. If you kill me, you'll never find the key."

Anger flared in Hattie's eyes, and she spat, "Or, I could simply force you to tell me where it is," then lunged at Rosemary, shoving her backwards into the pool with a splash.

Rosemary kicked her way back to the surface with an effort, her skirts weighing her down and pulling her towards the bottom. With all her might, she managed to grab hold of the pool's edge and take a deep breath before she felt Hattie's hand on her head, pressing her back into the darkness.

"Where is the key?" she demanded, allowing Rosemary another gulp of air before dunking her under a third time.

As she struggled beneath Hattie's grip, Rosemary realized she might just be done for. She was tired, and she didn't know how much fight she had left. This was it, the end. She had overplayed her hand just like the Parsons had, and now she would pay for it—with her life.

Her life didn't flash in front of her eyes, but the faces of her loved ones did. Her brother, Vera, her parents, Max—they would all be devastated, and it was all because she couldn't simply leave the investigations to the professionals.

Rosemary was nearly out of air and beginning to fade when suddenly, the pressure of Hattie's vice-like grip lessened, and she bobbed up enough to get in another breath. The sound of a commotion reached her ears, but she was sputtering too hard to tell what it was.

"Rosie!" It was Vera's cry that rent the air. Rosemary's eyes fluttered open long enough to discover she'd been rescued after all. Desmond held Tony, who didn't look like he was putting up much of a fight, while Frederick—nail marks on his cheek—restrained a struggling Hattie. And Vera—well, Vera was focused on one thing: her dearest friend, who was in trouble, and who she would do anything in her power to save.

"Rosie," Vera shouted again. She jumped into the pool, couture dress, shoes, and all and, with a burst of adrenaline-fueled herculean strength, grabbed Rosemary around the waist and heaved her up towards Molly's waiting arms.

More capable than expected, the stewardess hauled Rosemary out of the water and dumped her rather unceremoniously on the edge of the pool.

"Are you all right?" Vera rose from the water like a siren from the sea, her hair slicked back to show dark eyes above slanting cheekbones.

"I'm fine." Rosemary coughed up a dribble of water, looked down at her bedraggled self, then back at Vera. Some things in life just weren't fair. Then her gaze tracked back to Hattie, who still struggled in Frederick's less-than-gentle embrace.

Heat rose up to beat back the chill of still-dripping pool water, and for once, Rosemary didn't bother to bank the fire of her rage. Had she but realized it, when she approached Hattie, she was fury to Vera's siren and every bit as glorious.

Usually, it was Vera who got to set aside her genteel decorum, but this time it was Rosemary who was incensed enough to resort to physical retribution. In a move that surprised even her friends, she pulled back her arm and punched Hattie Humphries in the eye. "That's for trying to drown me." Her fist struck a second blow. "And that's for forcing my friend to ruin her dress."

The sound of running feet preceded Captain Hughes' entrance and that of several stewards behind him. Frederick and Desmond had to take over the explanation of what Hattie had been doing before he finally listened, but in the end, he ordered, "Take them to the brig."

Rosemary raised a brow. "I guess you don't have room for me in there anymore, do you, Captain Hughes?"

Chapter Twenty-Nine

When Rosemary and her friends were finally alone in the staff staircase just off the stewards' quarters, Frederick enveloped his sister in a brotherly hug that warmed her to the bone. "Don't you ever do anything like that again, Rosie. Do you hear me?"

"I promise, Freddie," she said, pulling away, "but I have to go and talk to Mr. Tait right now. I think—I think he might have murdered Dolph." It was a conclusion she had come to somewhere in the midst of everything that had happened because, well, it was the only conclusion that made sense—except it didn't make sense, not completely.

"What?" Desmond asked, his mouth hanging open. "Mr. Tait? He's the most docile man in the compartment." Vera's expression said she agreed wholeheartedly.

"I know," Rosemary said slowly, "but he's the only one who could have done it unless the far-fetched idea that the trap was set while we were docked in Southampton is true I just can't believe that's the case. Not when there's other evidence to consider."

Rosemary explained what she'd learned from little Rose and the gist of her conversation with Trix McCoy. "Mr. Tait and Dolph had some sort of altercation, and shortly after that, Dolph turns up dead. In between, the notebook was lost or, more likely, stolen. I have a bad feeling they're all connected."

"Assuming you're correct," at Rosemary's raised brow, Frederick qualified, "which of course I am, what could Dolph have done to push a nice man like Mr. Tait to commit murder? Des is right; he's just not the type."

"I think it has something to do with Trix McCoy's next novel," Rosemary replied. "Although, I think her theory of a crazed fan is a bit fantastical. Mr. Tait certainly wouldn't fit that description."

Desmond reached out and touched Rosemary's arm, his eyes alight with excitement. "Perhaps not a crazed fan, but how about a rival writer? Mr. Tait has a typewriter in his stateroom. Perhaps he's an aspiring author as well."

Aspiring author. The words reverberated through Rosemary's head. She remembered what Trix McCoy had told her about Dolph. Few friends, some family in Devon, and a former employer who was, as Dolph had described, a bit of a wet blanket. The description could certainly be applied to Mr. Tait.

"Oh my goodness! He's Dolph's old boss—the unpublished author, the one with *excellent ideas but no drive or execution*." Miss McCoy's words came rushing back. At the time, Rosemary hadn't given much thought to which of the two types of writers Trix McCoy considered herself, but now Rosemary realized she was one of the ones who *lacked the creativity necessary to capture an audience*.

Even Dolph himself had said, on the last night of his life, that Miss McCoy had taken a snippet of an idea and turned it into a complex story. Why that would anger Mr. Tait so much was still vague in her mind, but she knew she was onto something.

"Where is my handbag?" she asked suddenly, another snippet of the evening rising to the surface of her memory. "I need my dinner menu."

Vera, carrying both her own and Rosemary's handbags over her sopping-wet dress, passed it over. Water dripped out of the handbag, and Rosemary's spirits sank.

"Will mine help?" Desmond asked, producing his dry one.

Rosemary unfolded the menu with shaking hands, and her heart sank when her fears were realized. "Mr. Tait is from Devon," she said, "as was Dolph, and you all know how I feel about coincidences."

"Uh, Rosie, do you remember who followed Miss McCoy to the lifts after dinner?" Frederick asked, serious for once.

She did remember seeing Dolph retire just after Miss McCoy did, and then Rosemary remembered something else. "Oh no. I told Mr. Tait that she'd found another of Dolph's notebooks. We need to hurry!"

Up they went, exiting the staff staircase on D Deck and circumnavigating the packed dining saloon. The Verrattis' farewell performance was in the offing, and passengers milled about everywhere. Getting to an open lift took longer than Rosemary would have liked, but she was relieved to discover the B Deck corridor virtually empty.

Still in her wet clothes, Rosemary strode to Miss McCoy's door and knocked urgently. "Trix, are you in there?" she called, hearing no reply. Again she knocked, harder, and could swear she heard a muffled squeak coming from inside the stateroom.

"Excuse me, ladies and gentlemen," Stratford's voice came from the direction of the stewards' station. "Is there some assistance I can offer?" Had the moment been less dire, Rosemary would have been amused or perhaps impressed by his ability to maintain professionalism in such an odd setting.

"We need this door open, now," she demanded, "or we'll break it down." Unlike the day when Dolph's body was discovered, he didn't stare at Rosemary incredulously but instead quickly pulled a set of keys out of his pocket and did as he was asked.

When the disheveled group tumbled into Miss McCoy's stateroom behind Stratford and Rosemary's eyes absorbed the tableau laid out before her, she realized without a doubt that her assumption had been the correct one.

Mr. Tait sat on one padded armchair, Miss McCoy across from him on another. In between them on a low coffee table sat a slightly tarnished tea tray holding two empty glasses and a suspicious-looking stoppered bottle. It wasn't painted with the word *poison* or a skull and crossbones, but it was clear enough to Rosemary that it didn't contain cough syrup.

The expression on Miss McCoy's face was one of abject horror, while Mr. Tait appeared quite serene and, in fact, positively smug. It was a similar madness to that which Rosemary had seen in Hattie's eyes, and she could feel her heart start to beat out of her chest.

"What's going on in here?" Stratford, the only one with an official capacity, demanded in a voice only marginally less professional than the one he'd used outside—a feat, in Rosemary's eyes. His gaze traveled from the coffee table to the credenza on the opposite side of the space and lit upon a second silver tea tray. "That's the missing tray!" Stratford exclaimed. "I've been looking everywhere for that!"

His mouth clamped shut as the implications sunk in—not only for the murder but also for speaking to passengers out of turn.

"He killed Mr. Sutton," Rosemary explained, her eyes never leaving Mr. Tait's face. Even though she had only met him five days prior, she had felt a connection with the man—a sort of father-daughter camaraderie and a level of respect that had now plummeted through the floor and into the depths of the sea below her feet.

Miss McCoy didn't get up or attempt an escape, nor did Mr. Tait. He shifted in the seat, crossed his legs, then admitted, quite frankly, "Yes, I killed Dolph, and I suspect if you know that you also have an inkling as to why. Miss McCoy doesn't seem to, which is a pity. Perhaps I've overestimated her mental capacities—and underestimated yours."

"Why?" Miss McCoy demanded, her terror turning to rage at the unnecessary insult.

Desmond added as he stepped forward, "I'd also like the answer to that question." He had his own reasons for feeling betrayed by Mr. Tait.

The man turned and, with sincere sadness, eyed Desmond. "I'm sorry to disappoint you, young man. If I'd had my way, you'd have remained none the wiser. I simply couldn't let her publish another one of my ideas."

He turned then and met Miss McCoy's gaze, which

had run the gamut of emotions to settle into one of understanding and disappointment. "You were his former employer."

That part of the story Rosemary had already gleaned, so the meaning behind Mr. Tait's comment dawned on her a few moments before it did Miss McCoy. When it did, when the author's eyes lit with the full realization that her plots—or stories, or whatever she wanted to call them—had been Mr. Tait's ideas first, she looked as though she might go even madder than he.

"You—Dolph—no!" Miss McCoy sputtered to Mr. Tait's delight.

"You're a fraud," he replied, still quite calm. "A double fraud, I'd say, since it seems Dolph left even you in the dark. He might still be alive if he had been truly remorseful and agreed to my conditions. Unfortunately, he defended himself and you, spouting all that nonsense about you having taken my *snippet of an idea* and turning it into a masterpiece."

Evidently, those words had stuck in Mr. Tait's mind as well as Rosemary's. She couldn't blame him for being angry; that must have felt like a slap to the face. Still, it didn't justify murder!

"You won't be doing it again." Mr. Tait addressed Miss McCoy directly, the madness twisting his lips into a sneer. "She won't steal my work again." He turned to Rosemary. "I've taken care of that well enough." His gaze tracked to the bottle on the table, but his words came out slurred.

"In point of fact, you haven't." Trix McCoy stood to her full height, dwarfing Mr. Tait as she loomed over him. "I don't know what you put in my glass, but you should have paid more attention if you wanted me dead. While you paced and ranted, I swapped the glasses."

In a matter of moments, Mr. Tait was gone, and there had been nothing anyone could do to stop it. He'd earned his death whether it came at the end of a rope or by his own hand.

"I will alert Captain Hughes," Stratford said, sorrow evident in his voice, "and fetch Molly for Miss McCoy."

The author looked less the worse for wear than she had after Dolph's death, and Rosemary suspected that for quite a while she would bask in the knowledge that his killer had been put to justice before the weight of what had just transpired fully hit her. Or, perhaps she would prove more resilient than that, after all.

"Is there anything else I can do for you?" Stratford asked. If he was fazed, he did an excellent job hiding the fact.

After a murmur of 'no thank yous', Rosemary said, "You can forgive us for suspecting you of several nefarious deeds. We . . . I misjudged you terribly."

The color rose in Stratford's cheeks and his blush deepened when Molly appeared in the doorway and overheard the words of praise. "I heard a commotion," she said, taking the pressure off Stratford to answer Rosemary's question. Instead, he merely nodded gratefully and returned to the matter at hand.

CHAPTER THIRTY

All Rosemary wanted was to change into dry clothes, go to bed, and wake up the next morning knowing New York City was only a handful of hours away. What she really wanted was to get off the ship and work out a way to sprout wings and fly home.

If anything would cause her to remain in the States for an extended period, it would be her desire to avoid another journey across the sea! After her experience, she thought it quite likely she would side with her mother the next time the discussion of transatlantic travel was broached.

Unfortunately, the expression—or rather, the pout—on Vera's face changed her mind. After all, her friend had jumped into the pool to save her while wearing her most coveted couture dress. The least Rosemary could do was make herself presentable and suffer through the Verrattis' performance.

Really, it wasn't such a hardship. While she waited,

patiently for once, for Vera to finish primping, Rosemary picked up a copy of that morning's *The Atlantic Edition* that she had yet to peruse.

New York City anxiously awaits the arrival of three very special celebrities: bestselling lady mystery author Trix McCoy, and the incomparable singing duo of Mirella and Gianni Verratti! But, ladies and gents, if you want to see them together, you'd better get your tickets now; it seems the golden couple has decided to part ways, and their performance at The Cotton Club is slated as their farewell show. It's sure to be a sellout!

Curious, Rosemary thought to herself. The breakup had only occurred the previous evening, in the middle of the sea, and yet the press had got hold of it in time to report it in the morning papers.

Running a bit late, the foursome had just settled into their seats when the room went dark and a lone spotlight fell on Mirella Verratti. As one, the audience breathed in on a sigh that held for a moment until the first chord struck.

The singer lifted her chin, closed her eyes, and released a sound so pure, it raised the hairs on the back of Rosemary's neck. A few seconds into the song, another spotlight flashed on Gianni Verratti's face as he stood some way back and to the side of the woman he'd soon be leaving behind.

Ever so slowly, Mirella turned towards her husband,

tilted her head, and put everything she had into the words of the love song they'd made famous together. Equally slowly, he moved closer, and closer still until the song finished with the couple in a near embrace. Gianni Verratti gazed down at the breathless perfection of his wife's face and smiled.

That had been no performance. The look was one of great affection, Rosemary was certain. She recalled all the encounters she'd had with the pair, and all the things she'd overheard, and she almost wished the Parsons were still into gambling. Given the chance, she would put everything she had on the Verrattis' public fight being the performance and the depth of caring between them during this song genuine.

Then, Rosemary caught another loving glance—this one between Mr. Verratti and the male journalist who had been following him and his wife all over the ship. It was fleeting, but it was all the confirmation she needed.

Perhaps it had been a sham all along, or perhaps Mr. Verratti was the love of Mrs. Verratti's life—the one who she would never forget, but either way, Rosemary knew the singer had sacrificed something of herself, of her own happiness, to ensure he would be able to live life to the full.

Rosemary could understand why Vera had been so enamored of Mrs. Verratti, and she had to admit, she felt exactly the same way.

EPILOGUE

On the way to breakfast in the Winter Garden Lounge the next morning—the last morning—Frederick teased his sister. "What will Max say when he finds out you didn't even make it off the boat without singlehandedly solving another murder?"

"Singlehandedly?" Desmond took mock offense. "I helped."

"By telling me about a typewriter?" Rosemary smiled and patted him on the arm. "Is that how you "helped" solve that crime in America, too?"

Desmond declined to answer.

So much had changed since the very first time they'd all dined together. For one thing, the group was smaller now, with only Rosemary and her friends, the Long family, and Miss McCoy.

The deaths of both Dolph and Mr. Tait weighed on the remaining passengers, but the mood bone of acceptance or, at least, resignation. In contrast, nobody felt particularly sorry that the Parsons hadn't made an appearance or for Hattie Humphries—especially Rosemary, who Hattie had attempted to make fill the last empty coffin left in the cargo hold.

Across the table, Mrs. Long tended to her two girls while gazing wistfully across the room where a hand of bridge was being dealt. When she caught Rosemary's eye, she looked away guiltily. It seemed the lady had yet to learn her lesson. Rosemary shook her head ruefully and hoped for Mr. Long's sake she would exercise more caution in the future.

He—Mr. Long—sat next to young Stewart, leafing through a comic with genuine interest. The boy's eyes were bright when they caught Frederick's gaze, and he winked.

"Mrs. Lillywhite," little Rose Long called, leaning over the empty chair between herself and Rosemary and pulling her sketchbook from beneath the table. She leafed through until she found the portraits of Rosemary and Vera, tore the sheet carefully from the book, and presented it with a shy smile. "This is to say thank you."

"You're most welcome. Would you mind if I looked at the rest?"

Rosemary opened the cover and leafed through the contents, a tear coming to her eye. "These are—these are simply beautiful," she said with emotion. On the pages, the talented little girl had sketched what felt like every nook and cranny of the ship.

Handing the book back, Rosemary said, "You must promise never to stop looking at the world around you and always draw from the heart. That is the mark of a true artist." Little Rose bobbed her head, then waved goodbye as her parents had finished breakfast and were now ready to return to their stateroom.

"Won't our children be lucky to have such a champion as their Auntie Rose?" Vera said, elbowing Frederick and tossing a grin in his direction.

Evidently, she'd come to some sort of conclusion about such things without Rosemary's help, or perhaps Vera was simply speaking of an indeterminate future, but Rosemary nearly keeled over with laughter when Frederick's face drained of all color, and he gulped several times.

Uncharacteristically silent throughout the meal, Trix McCoy let out a snort. "It's no mystery what's got under his skin, is it?"

"Speaking of which," Rosemary said, taking the pressure off her brother. "Have you decided to go ahead with Dolph's final plot?"

Miss McCoy pursed her lips briefly and shook her head. "Heavens, no. As it happens, I've been thinking of going with something a little closer to home. After all, how often does one have a murder dropped right in one's lap?"

"You're planning to write about Dolph's death?" Rosemary frowned at the notion of exploiting the nice man's death for the sake of Miss McCoy's career. Then she looked at the other woman's face, saw the sorrow underlying forced cheerfulness there, and decided to consider it a tribute instead.

"You'll be in it, of course," the author said as though Rosemary ought to be grateful.

This time, Rosemary's frown came with a head shake. "Oh, I don't think that's necessary. Your Mrs. Willoughby should be the one to solve the crime."

"The hell she should." This from Vera, of all people. "It should be you, Rosie, and she should call it *Mrs. Lillywhite Investigates: A Murder in First Class.*"

Desmond shook his head. "Certainly not. If you want to appeal to the everyman, best not to mention class distinction right in the title. Perhaps just *A Murder on Board.*"

"For heaven's sake," Rosemary exclaimed. "Don't I get a say in this? Perhaps I don't *want* my name on a series of murder mysteries!"

"How about, *A Death at Sea?*" Vera suggested excitedly, "And you're more than welcome to include my likeness in the novel if you're so inclined. I do love to see my name in print! It's almost as thrilling as having it emblazoned in lights!"

Frederick ignored the stars in his wife's eyes and said

dispassionately, "You're all wrong. If you're going to write this story, Trix, you absolutely must call it *Mrs. Lillywhite Investigates: Evil on the High Seas*.

Made in the USA
Las Vegas, NV
09 April 2024